Paul Smaïl is a pseudonym for the author who now lives in Morocco. A second novel, *Casa, la casa*, was published in 1998.

SMILE

A Novel

by
Paul Smaïl

Translated by
Simon Pleasance & Fronza Woods
with Janine Dupont

Funded by
THE
ARTS
COUNCIL
OF ENGLAND

Library of Congress Catalog Card Number: 99-63335

A catalogue record for this book is available from
the British Library on request

The right of Paul Smaïl to be identified as
the author of this work has been asserted by him
in accordance with the Copyright, Designs
and Patents Act 1988

First published by Editions Balland, Paris, 1997

First published in English in 2000 by Serpent's Tail,
4 Blackstock Mews,
London N4 2BT

Website: www.serpentstail.com

Typeset by Avon Dataset Ltd, Bidford on Avon,
B50 4JH

Printed in Great Britain by Mackays of Chatham plc,
Chatham, Kent

10 9 8 7 6 5 4 3 2 1

To my brother

Author's Note

This book is a novel. Any resemblance between events and persons described in it and real events and persons is purely coincidental.

To preserve the *Barbès Arab* flavor, Arabic expressions have been deliberately loosely transcribed, the way they sound.

'So disordered, self-condemning is his look, that had there been policemen in those days, Jonah, on the mere suspicion of something wrong, had been arrested ere he touched a deck.'

Moby Dick, Herman Melville

— You can call me Smaïl

I insisted, drawing the word out, leaving a good gap between the 'a' and the 'ï' with its two dots: Smy-eel. It had been a while since I'd pronounced my name the Arab way. Or, rather, it was ages since I'd spat my name out the Arab way, clearing the 's,' the 'm,' the 'a,' the 'ï,' and the 'l' from the depths of my throat. I usually cheat a bit and pronounce it the stylish English way, aspirating like the English do, all posh, and smiling: *Smile*. But what's it all about? Then it strikes me that the employer I'm calling is smiling too, on the other end of the line. And since my father had the bright idea of giving me a very ordinary Christian first name, when he registered my birth at the 18th *arrondissement* city hall in Paris, on May 5, 1970, I can kid myself by introducing myself this way. Then it's just a question of reeling off my useless track record without drawing breath: high-school gradua-tion plus five years at university, that's it. Yeah, arts degree. Comparative literature . . . Uh-oh! The smile at the other end of the line is already freezing. Let's not talk about CVs. I'm not going to list the three or four casual jobs I've had while waiting . . . Waiting for what? Because, let's face it, there won't be any real job for me, either because my degree doesn't at all qualify me for the job on offer, or because I can only get so far by being crafty, rubbing out those two dots on the 'ï' and touching up my photo, I can get an interview, but sooner or later I've got to

1

show up in the flesh ... An A-rab, in other words. Nig-nog, *beur*,* A-rab, rat, raghead, *sidi*,† darkie, wog – take your pick. Short back and sides, shiny loafers and a silk tie won't get me anywhere. Smile, Smaïl ... Paul or whatever ... There'll always be another applicant less swarthy than me, hair less frizzy, skin not so rough, nose less hooked.

Berber beauty, Myriam said with her lovey-dovey eyes. But I wasn't born yesterday. And the boss even less so. The worst of the lot are human resource types. They've got your number straight off, sniffing you out like dogs trained to do just that. They've got the eye, all right. I'm not a human resource; my mug's too ugly. End of story.

North Africans who try to be taken for white are like those German Jews who, before the war, thought they could pass. The only people they conned were themselves. A false nose sticks out even more than a real nose in the middle of your face. And we're at war. And we'll be discarded, one way or another. If not exterminated.

My brother doctored his ID card. No big deal, just a tiny ink blot that – mum's the word – turned the two dots over the 'i' into one big dot. And he had his hair dyed. Ash blond, but it was too light to fool anybody – a way of putting the dots back on his 'i's without him realizing it. When I went into his room in the *Krankenhaus*, that was the first thing that struck me: His hair had grown back, and grown back black, of course. Against the white pillow, his face, all skin and bone and hollow with pain, had turned back into the face of an A-rab, an old A-rab

* A young North African born in France
† A North African immigrant living in France

from the Rif, dry, scrawny, and bony. The guy from the Rif, who doesn't give up so easily, the pious Muslim who's never drunk a drop of wine in his life, the good soldier: Ahmed Smaïl, father of our father, in the only portrait we've still got of him, the black-and-white ID photo, yellowing now, shown on his French Army military record, with that little metal ring boring a hole in his forehead, like some ominous sign about how he would be killed at Ulm. A loyal subject. A credit to the motherland, oh yes ... I remember how, in the death camps, they called Muslims the ones who were handed back on the point of dropping, sure to die before long. The skin would wrinkle and turn duller, the eyes glazed over ... As soon as I saw him, I knew he was done for, and it wouldn't be long, either. Two thin vinyl tubes vanished into his nose like worms up a corpse's nasal passages. His body, which he'd shaped so powerfully by pumping iron, his body that he had tortured and shown off such a lot, his body now seemed weightless, disembodied. Sheets and blankets concealed his bulky muscles, or what was left of them. He'd become a wog once more, and a child. My kid brother, the skinny little guy I used to read to at night, before lights out, a few pages of *Treasure Island* or *Moby Dick*.

I wasn't allowed to kiss him. Besides, how could I possibly kiss him? Visitors had to wear a face mask. I stroked his cheek, but all my fingers could feel was the cold rubber of the obligatory gloves I also had to wear, and it made me shudder. I was on the verge of tears. All I could think of to say was: 'Poor Queequeg!' A nickname I once gave him.

When the statutory ten minutes were up, the nurse's

eyes told me the visit was over. I left the sterile tent, looked back over my shoulder, and watched the veil of see-through plastic fall gently back into place at the foot of his bed. It was like placenta and shroud all at once, and behind it he was nothing more than a ghostly shadow, barely human. One thing at least: He would never be a human resource ... And neither would I. That's what came into my mind then, though God only knows why.

In the elevator I swore solemnly that I'd finally get down to the book I'd promised myself I would write, the book I'd promised Daniel. So I wouldn't be wasting any more time looking for a job that fitted my qualifications, a job I'd never find. Because I didn't want to teach and because I was fed up always being turned down and turned away. Because I'd had it with being humiliated, most of all, just like he'd spent too long being humiliated by begging for work, a part-time job, a course. 'Anything,' he would say, 'anything!'

I'd be a writer, nothing less. All I needed was enough to live on ... enough to survive, at least. I'd keep on delivering pizzas, in the evenings. And Mr Luis would surely find me a night watchman's job somewhere, the way he always managed to do for his boxers. Night watchman: What better for someone hell-bent on becoming a writer – and nothing else?

Night watchman. Caretaker of the night, in a way. With that heady feeling of having hours ahead of you, and having them all to yourself. Stronger than a feeling: a sensation. The real sensation of time passing, of time's substance, its density and weight. Its reality, in a word. This is what real time is. Not the split-second thing of share values all over the world, not sporting feats broadcast live to TV viewers the world over, but the silence and solitude, here, at three in the morning. The felt-tip pen squeaking across the lined paper. Words coming one after the other. Sentences one after the other. One after the other, the sheets of paper covered with black writing from top to bottom. And to be able to say to myself, I've got all the time in the world.

I'm writing. I'm writing as things come to me, any old how, as my pen and my memories dictate. I don't cross much out. By day, when I've had a few hours' sleep, I clean up the jottings I made the night before on my notepad. I key it all in.

The next night I take up where I left off. Now and then I look up for a few moments, checking on the screens that everything is cool on board: nobody in the corridors, nobody on the stairs. Above me, those grunts and shrieks of pleasure that I've got so used to, I don't even notice them anymore . . . So I turn a new page of my pad. And start from the top.

I don't really know where I'm going. I still don't know if all this will end up making a book, or if it will be a novel or my life, give or take a little. We'll see. It's an adventure. Looking for the white whale . . . Setting sail by night. Weigh anchor! Cast off! Furl the foresails! Lower the spanker! Hoist the jib and the flying jib! Hug the wind! Hug the wind! Ready about! Heave-ho! Haul in the sails! Furl! Luff! Head wind . . . *Inch' Allah*!

On the wall opposite, a flickering mauve neon tube traces the word *Night*, and the halo of light is reflected on the wet tarmac of Rue des Martyrs. On the glass here I can read *Le Modern'* the wrong way round. There are still sticky traces of the final 'e' that the previous hotel owner pulled off and replaced with an apostrophe, thinking it would look more – you guessed it – modern, or more chic. But he didn't have a chance to feel good for long about how he'd modernized the premises and the name. A couple of days later they found him face down in a pool of blood . . . A grim tale that I'm not meant to know about, and least of all from the lips of Mr Luis.

But *Le Modern'* isn't such a seedy joint. It's not, strictly speaking, a whorehouse. Its clientele includes middle management, locals, people from out of town, and foreigners on business trips who want to get it off with an office colleague or some part-time lady of the night. Rooms by the hour, by the day, and by the night . . . But no resident whores staying there all year round. The boss won't have that. Nothing too sordid, nothing too weird: linoleum flooring, minimal furniture all in chipboard and mock leather, washbasin/bidet/shower/WC all in one unit. Walls hung with flesh-pink rubberized padding, bedspreads of blood-red chenille – Péquod claims this excites the trick. Condoms in the bedside table – Péquod makes it his business to restock them. And the reception area, with its washable silvery wallpaper, all very trippy.

The first night I reported for duty here, I thought I'd go crazy if I kept staring at those pink diamonds and those obsessive orange sunbursts. But you get used to anything. And I also got used to the moans and cries coming from the TV room on the first floor, where a multiload VCR played nonstop adult movies. This week: *The Diabolical Dick*, *Once Upon a Time in the Ass*, *Bitches Fuck Together*, *Screw Me*.

Closed-circuit video cameras, one in the lounge, one on each floor, one in the elevator, two in the stairwells, dramatize the perspective of the empty corridors filmed from above. And on the monitors, where the blurred black-and-white picture flickers, you'd think you were in a thriller with something dramatic about to blow at any minute. Violence.

But nothing happens. Most of the time, nothing happens. A john bawling out a lot of drunken rubbish or puking in the corridor. Another, too out of it to fit the key in the lock, but I see him punching the poor woman with him when she gives a try. A novice sado calling for help because he can't loosen the straps he's tied round his slave. Two Dutch guys swearing at a poor Greek fellow quietly jerking off in the lounge in front of *Screw Me* . . . Little things like that. In the three months I've worked as night watchman at *Le Modern'*, I've intervened only six or seven times. I put down my notepad and my felt-tip, lock the outside door, run upstairs, read the riot act, run back downstairs, and pick up where I left off:

— The sea, kids!

It was still little more than a vague blue shimmer in the distance, but it grew bigger and bigger as the train sped closer.

— Where? Where? Daniel shrieked.

He folded his knees under him to appear taller, and looked pleased as punch. The dazzle unfurled halfway up the carriage windows, as the track ran parallel with a beach. A sailboat changed tack, leaning elegantly with the wind. Way over there, invisible on the other shore, lay the land of our forebears, with its white towns, its palm groves, deserts, mirages, oases, and its magic ... Respectful of the property of the French Railway Company, for which he worked and was a model employee, my father gave my brother a little tap across the knees and got him to sit up properly. Especially as that seat was covered with fabric – we were proudly traveling first class ... Then I heard this contemptuous sigh. Turning round, I saw, on the other side of the aisle, an elderly middle-class couple staring at us, full of hatred, with *Le Figaro* magazine spread between them on the armrest showing the July 14 parade on the cover. All these details are still etched in my mind, the woman in her candy-pink suit, the man trembling with his Parkinson's disease, the way they both pursed their lips, nostrils quivering as if they were overcome by our smell. In different circumstances they would have denounced us and sent us to our death.

The fun of discovering the sea had vanished. And Daniel started to cry, but our parents did not know why.

What now? Nothing. A bunch of skinheads rushing along Rue des Martyrs screaming:

— We won! We won!

For emergencies, there is an alarm on the floor connected to the 18th *arrondissement* police station. But when Péquod took me on, he made it clear that he would rather that I not use it. I should only ever use it as a last resort. From the way he said it, it would be better if I got myself killed rather than use it. I'd been recommended by Mr Luis, and I'd better not let him down – Péquod's threatening tone of voice was at once insinuating and indifferent, like baddies in TV serials.

He's provided me with a cosh, a dog-whistle, a marker gel and a stun spray, and he's paying me three-quarters under the table, one-quarter declared, so he stays within the fateful limit of sixteen hours a week, below which the employer is exempt from social security contributions. A more or less illiterate Pigalle whorehouse-keeper knows as much about all that as the boss of a conglomerate when it comes to milking some government loophole and beating the system. In any case, the way he deals with the tax people and the cops is something I personally don't want to know about.

The cash register is actually the biggest danger – me getting held up at gunpoint for a grand or two. At *Le Modern'*, nobody pays by credit card or check. As Péquod puts it, you pay upfront: no money, no goods. Lire, pounds, pesetas, florins, marks, dollars, they're all accepted here. So there's only cash in the drawer.

Even when I open it, I'm filmed too. I pull faces on purpose, giving a don't-mess-with-me look like the son-of-a-*harki** watchman I am, like a *beur* full of loathing. On my very second night on duty, I had the bright idea of hanging a pair of boxing gloves on the peg, the largest,

* An Algerian soldier who fought with the French in the Algerian war

9

an eight-ounce pair. I wear a pair of shiny black nylon Adidas pants, and a knock-off of a Death Squad sweater. And the heavy-duty bikers' boots Daniel left me, with their big buckles and protective pads that make a loud noise on the stairs . . . Yo, motherfucker, man! The wicked wog who'd fleece you for two cents!

The only way to get by in this life is to play a role. People don't want to know who you really are in this world, they want you to look as much as possible like the ready-made image they have of you . . . The way you might be in a TV movie. Take Péquod, for example. He dresses just like a pimp in an American TV series: tight-waisted stretch jacket with big shiny buttons, zip-up lilac shirt made of viscose, super-tight flares, and white cowboy boots that are so polished they look like imitation leather. The dandy of the Bronx. As seen on TV!

When I introduced myself to him, I saw right away in his eyes that I was almost a bit too clean. I'd dressed up as seriously as I could, with a tie and a splash of aftershave, and I was wearing my specs . . . A tough guy recommended by Mr Luis! He'd obviously expected the real tough guy who frightens people and smells of sweat – the real A-rab. He said to me:

– That's you, Smell?

He reads what he sees written, and he reads badly. So I pronounced my name the way it's spelled. Then, to play the game right, he had to fill out a bit of paper. I offered to help him fill it out, but I didn't push it, because I didn't want to hurt his feelings. Some Arab had just sold him a PC, with software for bookkeeping and mailmerge, half the list price before tax. Because he didn't know how to use it, Péquod had furiously

10

presumed that the hustler had palmed him off with a dud:

– I've had it up to my ass with dope and stuff.

Then he watched me sit in front of the screen, typing and clicking – *hafif*!

Someone other than Péquod would probably have felt slightly humiliated. But I didn't bother him at all, or so it seemed. He puts all his vanity into his gladrags and his gold baubles, the snakeskin case for his cell phone, the meshed foglights on his customized Cherokee. Since then I've realized that he doesn't respect me for my intelligence or my skills, but because I came recommended by Mr Luis.

Next day I borrowed his computer for four or five days to work on my book at home. Three months later, I still haven't given it back to him, but he appears to trust me – cut-and-paste – because I come recommended by Mr Luis.

Mr Luis's gym is located in a passage in the Batignolles neighborhood. For me, that's the north, and the westernmost limit of the known world. Apart from the faraway university called Paris-X, otherwise known as Nanterre, which I'd get to on the subway, my whole life, to date, has revolved around a territory bounded, roughly speaking, by La Fourche, La Chapelle, Le République, and La Trinité.

Barbès is where the action is. Between the Tati and Toto stores, on the fifth floor, overlooking the courtyard, that's where my aunt Zaïa lives. She put my parents and me up until my brother was born in 1973. In the other direction from the crossroads, you've got the pharaonic Luxor Palace cinema, where Leïla had her first unchaperoned date with her fiancé, Yacine. They went to see *Dr Zhivago*. Had I been a girl, they'd have called me Lara. France Bijoux, on the Boulevard de Magenta, is the jeweler's where my father-to-be bought their wedding rings; Face-to-Face, where my mother-to-be chose a romantic pearl-white satin wedding dress with chiffon trim; and Chamepeix Studio, where they had their picture taken, she sitting on a red velvet ottoman, he standing behind her, a hand resting on her shoulder. Rue Ordener, the new two-bedroom apartment that the family moved into when Daniel was born – Mum was opening the box containing her first set of dishes, knee-deep in a cloud of wood shavings that made her cough, when she felt the first contractions. Gare de l'Est and Gare du Nord, the rolling stock maintenance shops where my father ended up as a grade 10 supervisor. Between the Gare de l'Est and the Gare du Nord, Fernand Widal hospital, where he passed away. Boulevard de Clichy, the Sexyshow 2000, where I went to tell my brother that my father had died – I didn't recognize him straightaway behind the two-way mirror: In the red half-light, the black latex balaclava seemed to do away with his head, and he had put on a few more pounds of muscle. Boulevard Barbès, between the Star of Tunis and the Maghreb Sun, my bedroom, where I thought I'd wear out my sorrow by shadow-boxing – boxing the void. Hour after hour I boxed away in the empty space, sparring with my shadow on the wall . . . In the end, I was beaten.

I started boxing at thirteen. I was in my third year at the Jacques-Decour high school, and during every break, every single one, I got beaten up. And when school was over, they'd steal things off me. Everything went! My cap, my jacket, my backpack . . . And when I got home, I'd get an awful scolding from my father, who refused to believe I'd dared to stand up for myself, and my mum would sob, because she couldn't understand why her son – her son! youngest in the class! top of the form! – was forever being beaten up by the big shots.

Why? Because I was the youngest, and I got the highest marks. Because girls liked me. Because I was a bookworm. Because I didn't feel it was a disgrace to answer when the teacher asked the class a question. Because one day the French teacher read my essay out to the whole class, using it as a model. Because, like my father, I thought it was important to talk properly. To say, for example: 'It's that which I'm afraid of . . .' And not: 'It's that what I'm afraid of . . .'

I was afraid, sure. I lived in a state of constant fear. On the way to school, as soon as I saw the tops of the trees in the Square d'Anvers – the foliage, as I'd put it in my composition – 'Yo, motherfucker, the foliage, my ass!' – my gut would shrink, my mouth would go dry, and I was sweating. I'd swallow a mouthful of the special concoction my aunt Zaïa made for me to drink: homemade syrup that would make me constipated for three or four days.

My stomach was as hard as a rock and my knees turned to jelly. I'd see a whole gang of them on the sidewalk of Avenue Trudaine, just waiting to get at me and give me a sharp kick on the butt. The trueblood born-'n'-raised Frenchies would rib me because they'd decided I was too much of a *sidi* by half, the *sidis* would rag me because they reckoned I was too much of a Frenchie by half, the *pieds-noirs** would go for me because I was really neither a *sidi* nor exactly a Frenchie, the Blackos because in their eyes I was white, the Arabs and Vietnamese to get on the good side of the Blackos, the *sidis* and the Frenchies . . . Whenever I see a report on the TV news about the Hutus and the Tutsis, the school yard at Jacques-Decour high comes back to me. And the first person who comes on at me about how antiracist the young are, I'll let him have a left jab to the kisser. I can pack a good punch now, I know that much, and it just so happens I'm a southpaw! Kids are color-blind, yeah, right!

The worst thing was the harassment, the underhand tricks, blows below the belt, the slights behind your back, the sly blows – it can't hurt if nobody knows – burning my back with a lighter, slashing my anorak with a blade, and flicks on the back of the neck. And the gum stuck on my seat and covering my bag with graffiti, and the endless 'Asshole!'

Tariq, the leader of the gang, had nicknamed me Mistake . . . And his cronies would chant like a chorus:

– Yo! Mistake . . .

They would spit on me. I took refuge in the john. One day four of them cornered me in there, and Tariq tried to

---

* Colonial French born in Algeria

15

drown me by forcing me nose first into the overflowing toilet-bowl. I put up a struggle. The monitor who heard my bloodcurdling scream came in the nick of time, because I was choking to death. Then I threw up, I was so scared. He took me to the infirmary, but he seemed to think it was just an unfortunate little scuffle, nothing serious, whereas what it was was attempted murder, no more, no less. What's more, he advised me to keep my mouth shut. That way I wouldn't attract any more trouble:

– Calm down! You asked for it a bit, didn't you?

I started throwing up again. No longer from fear this time, it was because of a terrible feeling of injustice.

The gang was waiting for me at the gate, on the corner of Square d'Anvers. Five against one, and the one was smaller than them . . . Two of them grabbed me by the armpits, two more pinned me to the ground, Tariq ripped off my sneakers – brand-new Air Nikes. My Christmas present!

Not one passerby came to my aid, nobody saw anything. I felt like dying. I couldn't get to my feet. It was as if I was sinking into the sidewalk asphalt. And everything was swirling and pitching all around me, like on a heavy sea, the buildings, the trees, the sky, the railings round the square.

I had to walk home – the shame of it! – in my socks. Boulevard Barbès, Rue des Poissonniers, Rue Marcadet, Rue Ordener . . . When I reached our apartment block, I kept on going. And for a long time I wandered toward the marshaling yards before I decided to retrace my steps, climb the stairs, and ring the bell.

A neighbor on our landing saw me without any shoes on and said:

— Fucking hell, this isn't a mosque here, Paulou!

My father had just got home from work. I hardly managed to tell him what had happened to me, the words were colliding with each other inside me, and I was sobbing. He was livid, and he started to stammer. For once, he didn't accuse me of not standing up for myself; he took my word for it. He didn't let me put on another pair of shoes. Instead he grabbed me by the wrist, pulled me like a sack of something as far as the landing, and pushed me ahead of him into the elevator. He was going with me to ask the principal for some explanations and file a complaint at the police station. Behind the front door, Mum yelled something or other in Arabic, but he just shrugged his shoulders.

So I had to follow him in my socks. He walked fast, and I almost had to run to keep up with him. Blinded by my tears, with my wrist in his vice-like grip, bruised and hurting all over, I stumbled along. Rue Ordener, Rue Marcadet, Rue des Poissonniers, Boulevard Barbès . . . I got the impression everybody had their eyes riveted on my socks and that the passengers overhead in the elevated trains, rumbling along in a great din of light, were all staring down at me.

The principal couldn't see us. His assistant principal just promised halfheartedly that they'd be punished to make an example of them, and this Tariq fellow would be expelled. But since, for fear of reprisals or out of some misguided sense of honor, or both, I refused to name the names of the four other guys who'd jumped on me, he too ended up thinking I must have gone looking for trouble, or that maybe I was part of the gang. I claimed that I didn't know who they were because they'd taken me by surprise from behind. He suggested I should go and see the school shrink 'to verbalize my anxiety.'

My father was up in arms:

— Verbalize! That's the job of the police, verbalizing!

The assistant principal looked at him as if he was seeing a stain on the armchair:

— Calm down, Mr Smaïl! Calm down!

He can't have taken my father's threat to file a complaint seriously. He must certainly have known that people like us never go and file complaints with the police, that we never voluntarily enter a police station.

We both left the high school feeling humiliated. A shared shame bound us together just then. My father didn't grab me by the wrist again. Instead he laid a hand affectionately on my shoulder.

— You've got to learn how to defend yourself, he said. Come on!

He took me to the subway. It wasn't to go back home. My ordeal wasn't over yet.

We took the Porte Dauphine train, changed at Place Clichy, and got off at La Fourche. Then he led me to Mr Luis's gym.

How did my father come to know Mr Luis? He'd boxed a little himself, as an amateur, when he was younger.

The gym is at the far end of a dead-end street. You go down seven steps to get to it. On the left, white metal lockers and filthy showers, apparatus, wall bars, a lifting chair and a massage table, and benches for weights and dumbbells; on the right, the wooden floor, the ring, and some punching bags. Gray daylight, opaque like frost, falls from the louvre windows with their frosted panes, which give on to a street behind. People outside pass by like shadows, with their lives that, seen from inside, seem so simple. Their day is over, they buy bread and fruit, and they go home to their kids. Below, we're here to suffer, as Mr Luis is forever reminding us. And he'll invariably find a boxer to groan:

— This is hell!

A strong, confusing smell, a mixture of sweat, sawdust, wax, leather, resin, and ointment. The noise, too, the rapid rhythm of fists on punching balls, the slower, duller thwack of punching bags, the whistle of skipping ropes, soles squeaking in unison, people sniffing and catching their breath . . . As soon as a boxer stands looking at himself in a mirror, without thinking he starts breathing in and out harder, as if he wanted to be quite sure he was still breathing and not dead. His first adversary is himself, his reflection in the mirror, his double – fighting his nagging desire to throw in the towel there and then, and drop his guard.

Mr Luis belongs to the old school. He deals with us the hard way, always ready to curse us out, with the threat of sending us back to the changing room for anything we do wrong. Never a word of encouragement other than 'that's a little bit less lousy.' He reckons, in his Spanish brogue, that 'psy'holo'hy's a 'hing for sissies and faggots.' He was seven when he arrived in France, in 1939, on the shoulders of his Republican father, but he's never lost his Castilian accent. Nor his contempt, which is also very Castilian, for anything that, to his eye, was remotely to do with limp-wristed fags and homos – *maricones* – fancy, unconventional clothes, football shirts, designer sports-wear. So when we train, we all wear old gray fleece-lined cotton tracksuits, all flimsy and shapeless, like prison uniforms. And if we have to sweat our way back to our ideal weight, Mr Luis wraps us in big twenty-five-gallon garbage bags. A hole for your neck, two for your arms, three or four turns of heavy tape to keep it on your hips. Get outta here, you good-for-nothing, rubbish, reject. And if you dare complain, he'll stick a piece of that heavy brown tape across your lips too.

— Put a sock in it, kid! You're 'ere to 'ave a bad time! You're nothing but a piece of shee-it!

All of thirteen, terrified, and still in my socks, I watched how he roughly manhandled a huge black guy, with a haircut like a convict's, as he wrapped him in a garbage bag. And the black guy, who towered over him, just let him do it, and put up with his cursing without so much as turning a hair. I found myself thinking how harsh Captain Ahab was in *Moby Dick*. He scared me, but I was fascinated by this respect he inspired in guys who were much younger and, to all appearances, much stronger than he was.

I was also amazed by the nimble, quick way these guys lunged, dodged imaginary punches and the swinging movement of the bags, swiftly hopping from one foot to the other, attacking their shadows. They weren't fighting, they were dancing, and they seemed bent on defying gravity. I vaguely understood why boxing was known as the noble art. I told my father I really wanted to be like them, but that I was almost certainly too small.

Mr Luis answered that I could always start by learning the various positions and movements and the footwork. He said he'd make sure nobody hit me. He addressed my father like an old friend he hadn't seen for such a long time that he couldn't remember his name any more.

— Smaïl, Yacine. People have always called you 'mister,' Mr Luis.

I noted that while my father addressed him formally, Mr Luis was familiar back. They went to discuss terms in an office at the far end of the gym.

And that's when there was an outburst of hurrahs – the boxers were applauding one of their buddies, who was walking triumphantly down the stairs, his arms raised in a V.

— Djabril!

The night before, Djabril Benhaya had won his first title as French featherweight champion, and he'd come by ingenuously to receive his pals' congratulations. His Prince of Wales check jacket was a bit creased in front, because he unbuttoned it to show off his gold belt, shouting:

— Hip, hip, hooray!

Mr Luis emerged from his office again.

— What the hell's all this racket? Oh, it's you, Djabril! There's no need for all this hoopla, though. Get back to work, all of you!

But the featherweight champion, all flushed with his glory, and a bit puffy from the punches he'd taken on his face as well, strutted and twirled about, dodged uppercuts coming from nowhere, mimed that seventh round when he delivered the fatal right hook to his opponent . . .

— Hip, hip, hooray!

And then he turned toward me and, in the midst of all that laughter, put up his guard as if he was afraid it was my turn to lay into him, the way he'd laid into that poor Baby Habib. He asked me what I was doing there, if I was Mr Luis's new young hope.

— Go on! he said to me, brushing me lightly on the

chin with his right fist. Put your dukes up! Don't step back, fuck it! Are you a southpaw? Where you from, kid? A sand-nigger, like me, Djabril Benhaya. France wouldn't have any French champions if they hadn't had their colonies . . . Hey, what happened to your shoes?

Heedless of my acute sense of dignity, my father told him what had happened to me.

— Hold on, hold on, Djabril said to me. What size do you take?

I took sixes, like him. He went to his locker and came back brandishing a pair of black boxing boots with twenty-six holes!

— For you, buddy, they're for you!

Brand-new shoes, all leather. He hadn't even tried them on! Worth a fortune. But last night, out of superstition, he'd worn his old white pair. He'd remembered that he'd always won wearing white shoes . . . He hammed it up, with a happiness that was infectious, getting high on his show of generosity. He was playing the part of the archangel he was named after – Djabril . . . Gabriel.

My father told him I couldn't accept such a princely present – he used that very word, *princely*. Djabril was flattered and insisted. Said he'd be insulted if I refused. In the end my father gave in.

— And if you like, Djabril said to me, Monday morning, I'll take you to school! I'm your big brother. I'll straighten them out, you'll see! They won't dare mess with you after that. *Labès*? OK?

— *Labès*. OK.

I thought I was hearing things. He'd scribbled our address on the flap of a book of matches, as well as the time I left for school, except that he'd probably forget his promise and throw away the matches when he'd used the last one. He'd forget all about me – a French champion!

On Monday morning, though, who should I see, at the bottom of the apartment block, all smiles, his left eyebrow emphasized by an ironic pink strip of Band-Aid – Djabril! The archangel with the broken nose, casually leaning against a bright red Golf GTI. The top was down, and waves of disco music pulsated from the car.

– Get in, kid!

I snuggled into the bucket seat. The bass and percussion thumping in the speakers reverberated in my guts. Djabril pushed the REPEAT button and the singer panted like she was coming again and again – I love you, baby . . . I love you, baby . . . Her orgasm took over from the long last sustained chord . . . Seen through the tinted windows, Barbès turned into a triumphal boulevard. The tires growled at every traffic light. A pair of miniature boxing gloves, hanging from the rearview mirror, danced. And me, Paul Smaïl, I was the protégé of a French champion! *El-Djena*!

The faces of the cretins in Tariq's gang when they saw me slowly get out of the Golf GTI – spoiler, pierced rims, sun roof – and when they saw the window on the passenger's side lower electronically at the same time as they heard the quadraphonic sound, and when the French champion said out loud to me, in clear tones:

– If those sons of bitches fuck with you again, just let Djabril Benhaya know about it!

And in the gym, when I started carefully lacing up my all-leather, twenty-six-hole, black Everlast shoes . . . Woah! Dammit, asshole! I'm tripping! . . . Is this for real?

— He's got bottle.

That's about the one and only word of praise Mr Luis ever said about me. Having bottle means you can take those punches. It's rarely used for stylish fighters, usually for guys who fight with their guts.

Mr Luis also said I took it well. By that he meant that I wasn't scared, I didn't hide behind my guard, and I didn't drop to the floor with my first bruise.

I ended up at Jacques-Decour with people respecting me, even being afraid of me, even liking me. I didn't make a whole lot of friends at Mr Luis's. More or less all the guys wanted to turn pro at some time or other; they would hardly have a year of training behind them before they were already wanting to get into the ring, with their sights set on a career. Myself, I make it quite clear from the word go that I'm staying amateur amateur. And I know the way I repeat the word gets on their nerves a bit. For them it's like I'm posing. Whatever I do, I'll always be a wanker in their eyes. I don't necessarily turn up for the matches they have in Paris or the suburbs. I never go along when they have a fight out of town or abroad. If they draw lots, just by chance there's never a place for me. I pretend to be annoyed, just so's not to get on their wrong side, so they'll think I'm pissed off . . . Shit, bad luck, Paulou! . . . If they really knew how much I don't give a damn!

I'm not part of the gang; I keep my distance. I do just

enough so they don't treat me like a stuck-up prick, or a pain in the ass. Every now and then, the odd drink with them, at the corner bar, or a couscous at Farid's brother's place, a greasy spoon in the Impasse des Abbesses. The Royal Platter – lamb, spicy chicken and merguez sausage – for sixty-seven francs, a carafe of Boulâouane white for twenty-three, coffee on the house . . . When I've finished my coffee, I slip a hundred-franc bill under the wineglass and tell the others I'm off, gotta split. I don't make excuses and they don't ask. That's perfect! Nobody stops me.

I avoid the discussion. Their bellies full, the way they have, every single one of them, of launching into an argument that's as pointless as it is cantankerous: bikes, ass, chicks, God, WBA and WBC rankings . . . Whether Tyson's still number one . . . If the Koran forbids the use of rubbers . . . Whether all basketball players are faggots or not . . . If you need more balls to drive a bike than a Formula I car . . . If the Pope's a Polack . . . If Johnny's a Yid . . . If his real name is really Smet . . . The pitch gets louder, seeing who can out-shout who, who'll have the last word, or the killer argument. It's all a continual one-upmanship of insults, and mothers and sisters are all whores.

Fuck your race!

– *Na' din' mok*! Fuck your mother!

And all this so-called fraternity. We're all brothers. Around the big oval table, we could pose for a United Colors poster: *beurs*, Algerians and Moroccans, blacks, half-castes, and West Indians, a Yid . . . And even a thoroughbred French guy, just the one, with blue eyes. But the friendship between us is close to hatred. A certain animosity is always smoldering under the overly loud laughter and over-the-top displays of affection. High-fiving hurts, and those friendly slaps on the back of the head can floor you.

I leave Chez Mustafa, feeling empty inside, sick, stomach heavy. Under the green neon of the starry crescent on top of the gilded-glass door, I look waxen, scary. I curse myself for having once again put too much *harissa** in my soup. Sour taste of crushed chili, suppressed rage, lamb that's definitely mutton in this thief's place, mixture of resentment and anxiety . . . Feel like crying . . . yelling until I die . . . put it off. One thing's sure: I can't deal with this phony brotherhood anymore, their mean-spirited rivalries, their petty tyrant mentality, and their obsessive fear about being taken for faggots; queens! Virility and manhood are the only things they never tire of talking about: Who's got the longest dick, who's had the most pussy, who's got a foreskin and who hasn't . . . They can have a hard-on for hours, come fifteen times in a row, burst extra-large condoms because their dicks are so big – yeah, right!

Virility, and then religion ever since Fouad, Farid, Taouif, Samir-the-welterweight, and Samir-the-heavy-weight all started to play at being devoted Islamists, chanting to us, at the first excuse, the five or six suras they finally managed to memorize, refusing wine with much ado, hands raised – the Fascist salute, or as good as – waving away the kirs the owner wants to offer us.

— Stupid bastards! As if Arab pride meant looking like our caricature on TV!

That's what I let fly one night, infuriated, leaving the

* North African hot pepper sauce

26

table before the coffee came. After that they iced me for six months. Hello, goodbye, and keep a low profile! Who d'you think you are, jerk, eh?

Whatever happens I'll always be a gray to them. Someone suspicious. An outsider.

Anyway, I went on seeing Diop. He's the only real friend I've got in the gang, and I'm the only one who calls him by his first name: Bernard. At the table, he only opens his mouth to laugh mechanically at all their crap – ha-bloody-ha – chew his meat, lap up his soup, polish off the various dishes, and ask for second, third, even fifth helpings of semolina. When I get up to slip away, he often winks at me out of the corner of his eye to wait for him outside. He comes out a few minutes later. He likes walking back down toward Barbès with me. We talk about anything and everything, quietly, without insulting each other's mother at every turn . . . We just talk, you know. He asks me up to his pad for a joint, and to give me back the books I lent him, or lend me some of his. One time we had the lousy idea of exchanging books in the locker room at Mr Luis's gym. We took such a ribbing – 'Oh-ho! Faggots!' – that we never did that again. Literature seems to be an even more hazardous pleasure than smoking.

– I've had hash stolen now and then, but never my books, Diop jokes. Even the guys who stripped my pad bare left me my books.

Of all the novels I've lent him, his favorite, he tells me, is still *The Nigger of the Narcissus*. Was that me being provocative? Or maybe it was him? No. But just as the others call me gray, they call him Bounty behind his back: chocolate on the outside, coconut on the inside, black, white . . . Behind his back because he stands six feet two tall and weighs two hundred and ten pounds, and he's the hardest hitter on Mr Luis's team, and because he sometimes wears in his buttonhole, for a laugh – though nobody would dare laugh – a Bernard Butchers button, which says it all.

But he really fucked up the career Mr Luis predicted for him. In the ring, with the public all round, under the lights, he loses it. He becomes a mere shadow of the boxer he is. One night, at La Villette, on the third bell, we saw him returning to his stool, sobbing like a kid. He was lost, he didn't know what he was doing there anymore. Everybody booed and whistled and chucked empty cans at him . . . Mr Luis had thrown in the towel even before the referee declared him disqualified. Bernard Diop never boxed in public again.

He still goes to the gym three times a week. Out of habit? For fun? A bit of both, I guess . . . Like me. It's a ritual and a discipline, a religious practice, but a religion without any god. It's a way of squaring up against himself – Diop versus Diop. A way of sweating out hatred and anxieties. Whereas in fact he could not give a damn anymore about his weight, and just let himself go to seed, he'll sometimes ask Mr Luis for a garbage bag.

I remember the first time when I saw him wrapping himself in plastic like a piece of human garbage; he remembers me, a thin little kid, in socks.

And whatever happened to Djabril Benhaya?

A few months after his win, he got the shit beaten out of him in a nothing match in Brussels, against a half-wit from Luxembourg. KO'd in the first minute of round two. Embolism . . . Blind ever since. And yet he was wearing his white shoes . . .

The featherweight champion had just left Mr Luis for a coach with a better reputation. When Mr Luis heard about his accident, he muttered that he'd got what he deserved, that *hijo de puta* – son of a bitch. And we never heard him mention his name again.

My father made me go and visit him at the hospital. Djabril had been my guardian angel, and I owed him one. I promised I'd go the following Wednesday, but on the next three Wednesdays I found a lousy excuse each time and wriggled out of it. I'll confess, here and now, to a despicable lie: I told my father I'd been to the hospital, but I hadn't managed to see him, because visitors under fifteen weren't allowed in unless they were the blind man's kids ... The worst thing was, I was telling the truth and lying to him at the same time.

Then Djabril was allowed to go home to his parents' house, at Aubervilliers. I don't know how my father knew, but he reminded me of my promise. I lied again. The following Wednesday, I pretended I'd paid him a visit ... And what a strong impression that had had on me, seeing his dead eyes when he took off his dark glasses! and how courageous he was! and I'd read him a few pages of the book I'd taken along to fill the time on the train journey – *The Jungle Book*. And how he'd really appreciated it ... A whole novel! Without blushing, unhesitatingly, without drawing breath or contradicting myself. And looking straight back at Daniel, who might well have snitched on me, because we'd spent the afternoon together playing with some friends who lived in our block, two floors up.

So was I as good at telling perfect lies as the next person? And to my own father, what's more? Sure.

My father died without knowing that his son had lied to him. On one of my very last visits to the hospital, when he was still making sense, I wondered for a split second if I would ever have a clear conscience, even years later.

— Dad, there's something I . . .

— Yes?

— No. It's nothing. Just something stupid.

All of a sudden I thought that making that confession now would also be like admitting to him that he was a goner: You only ever make that kind of confession to people who are dying. Better to go on cheating, behaving as if he was going to get better and come home.

Heichma! Shame! I can hear my father, I can hear my mother, I can hear Aunt Zaïa spitting out the word the way you'd spit out a watermelon seed or a date stone. Shame has always seemed to me more shameful when it's said in Arabic. And my own personal shame stayed stuck in my throat – *heichma*! Is this why I write? On the back of my notepad I've jotted down these words by Jean Genet: *Writing is the last resort when you have betrayed*.

On a closed-circuit screen, an insomniac trudges along one of the corridors. As he gets closer to the camera, the angle distorts his features, like a fish-eye lens, flattening his face, stretching it until it makes him look alarmingly like an idiot. As if the third dimension had vanished.

I look away. And who do I see sticking out his tongue at me and squinting like a clown, his broken nose squeezed flat against the window, his face perfectly framed by the 'o' of *Modern'*? Diop. His fingertips drum a friendly hello on the glass, and I beckon to him to come in for a minute. But he makes signs that he is in a hurry to go to bed and that he can hardly keep his eyes open. Four in the morning, and he's just going back home to bed. And, always one for a laugh, though pretending to look stern, his finger is aimed at my notepad, ordering me to carry on writing.

Right. On we go. Actually, I'm turning back a page or two in my notebook. I'm coming back to the white-hot pebble beach, the midday dazzle on the sea. I'm rolling Captain Ahab's whaling ship toward the deep: a huge inner tube of a truck tire that my father mended to make a buoy for us. Daniel's got his sand bucket on his head, running around brandishing his spade.

— Stand by to board!

I tell him he's muddling up his stories, that we're going off to hunt Moby Dick. He objects, not without reason, that the white whale doesn't spawn in these parts. He'd be happier playing Treasure Island or The Mysterious Isle. Or else we'd be those fearsome Barbary Coast pirates who once scoured the Mediterranean and captured those Christian curs to turn them into slaves.

Ma calls to us to wet our hair first, and not stray too far from the edge.

— Me, I'm Sinbad! Daniel declares, splashing me with water, roaring with laughter.

Sinbad's his favorite hero ever since I gave him a picture book of his adventures for his tenth birthday. And why? Because the illustrator endowed the mariner of *The Thousand and One Nights* with a distinctively Arab look.

We get on board, squatting astride the great fat black rubber sausage dotted with patches, and sail toward the enchanted isle – the floating diving-board, yonder, where blond chicks who've taken their bras off loll about, giving me such a hard-on it busts the crotch netting inside my shorts.

Other brats on air mattresses and little inflatable dinghies try to sink us. But since I've been going to Mr Luis's gym for more than a year I've learned not to be afraid of anyone. A hefty punch let fly at the mattress or the front of the dinghy, and they tip over, one after the other, and the crews tossed into the sea all shout and laugh and splash about. Daniel's in seventh heaven, leaping about, cleaving the sky with his spade. Victory to the Barbary Coast pirates! We, the Smaïls, are the mightiest! We've repelled the attack from the king of France's privateers! *Allah akbar*!

We still let the current carry us toward the Enchanted Isle of Naked Chicks. We give it a wide berth. My plan is to go right round the pontoon and board it not by the ladder but up one of the anchor chains on the seaward side.

I appoint my brother skipper and hand our three-master over to him. I grab the chain all sticky with seaweed, and climb up it, trying not to let it creak. My chin's on a level with the tarred deck, and my nose and eyes open wide at all that flesh on offer, oily with sun lotion, pearly with sweat. God! Those breasts! Those nipples! Those tits! Those armpits! Those shoulders! Those bellies! Those thighs! The blond down on their thighs! And those vulvas barely hidden by wet bikinis! And the small of their backs, Lord! And those buttocks! And those dimples just where the buttocks start! Two of them, lying on their stomachs have stripped off their bottoms too! I'm oozing, I could come without touching them, I could come without touching myself!

But they've got a couple of hefty types with them, lurex mini-briefs and cool shades, bodybuilders' muscles, chunky chain bracelets, one with a solid-gold crucifix nestling in between his hairless pectorals, the other with a star of David . . . I haven't been quiet enough. They've propped themselves up on their elbows, and snarl at me:

— Beat it, jerk! No room here. And we don't want any runts peeping at us.

— And especially no *beurs*! Total apartheid here! And you, you stink like an Arab!

One of the mermaids shrieks with laughter, and that hurts me. Another squirts sun lotion in my eyes.

— Paul! Paul! Daniel calls from below, his voice hoarse with fear. Paul!

I wipe my eyes and pretend not to be intimidated, but the two fuckers with their big biceps have got up and are now threatening to hit me. This is no time to play hero, so I let go of the chain. I dive under the tire and come up in the middle. I say to Daniel:

— You're not scared, are you?

He says he isn't and shakes his head. But the way he looks, his silence, his lips, which he's biting so hard, say it all. Then I paddle hard with my feet to take him back to the beach. Like the white whale in the illustrations of *Moby Dick*, I noisily blow and spit out the water I've swallowed, but he doesn't find it funny anymore. He didn't unclench his teeth until that evening.

Even when Ma offered us ice creams, the stubborn kid remained silent.

— Chocolate and pistachio, Daniel? Three scoops, chocolate-pistachio-strawberry, Daniel? OK?

Speechless, he shook his head.
– What's the matter, baby?
She takes him in her arms to comfort him, but he pushes her away. He wants to be left alone.

Through the half-open door I can see her sitting hunched on a stool, her hands clasped about her knees, rocking gently back and forth, as if nursing her grief. She's not moaning anymore, or crying, and, for me, there's something even more awful about her stubborn silence than her heart-rending screams at the other end of the line when I called her from Hamburg to tell her once again what she already knew: that it was over.

She hasn't combed her hair. She's wearing a long, loose gown and slippers. Since my father died, Ma's much happier wearing Moroccan clothes – it's a way for her of not having to dress up anymore. Specially if she doesn't have to go anywhere. The fact is, she goes out less and less, and finds fewer and fewer reasons to leave the house.

Daniel didn't like her wearing her long gown – a gandoura – on the beach. I say Daniel, but if I'm totally honest with myself I should say: Daniel and I, her two sons. Even though one day, when my brother was getting at her for not wearing a dress like other women, I ticked him off severely:

– Fuck it, aren't you ashamed of yourself? Ma wears what she likes! You're lucky Dad didn't hear you.

I put the urn with his ashes on the upper bunk bed, his in the days when we shared this room. The uprights and the wooden ladder were the masts and shrouds of our ship. Hoist the mainsail! Furl the spanker and the royal! Aloft there, Queequeg!

On a shelf I find *The Adventures of Sinbad* and *Redburn: His First Voyage*. Stuck to the door, a full-length, life-size portrait of Vince Taylor, not the singer our parents listened to but the bodybuilder who won the 1992 Iron Man title. Above his bed – which once used to be mine – a poster from a Khaled concert. I don't remember him liking Khaled. I remember him listening to The Cure – *'This isn't love this isn't life this isn't real this is a lie ...'*

To stir things up, he would often say that he wasn't interested in anything Arab. But when he realized he was very ill, he stopped denying his roots. As if by becoming Arab he'd get better, maybe. Reading the Koran, listening to raï, deciding strictly to observe the next Ramadan ... Not much, really, and just for the form. And he died one moon before Ramadan. But he would definitely never have ticked Ma off again about her gown and slippers. At the very end, he said a strange thing, he said if he pulled through he'd go back to Morocco to live. Go back to live ... As if he'd ever lived there!

His toys are all still there. He kept everything, didn't break things, and looked after all his stuff. On his desk, piles of *Muscle World*, *Flex*, *Ironman* and *Hein Gericke* catalogs – with the pages devoted to cross-country biker gear marked with Post-Its. But also, neatly arrayed in three rows along the groove of the pen-tray, his Spidermen, his Goldoraks, his Darth Vaders and little Playmobil figures: workers, firemen, policemen, ambulance drivers ... And not one was without its accessories: helmet, tools, and first-aid box.

But most of them fall over when I open the top drawer. So was Daniel patient enough to stand them all up again every time? Or did he pull the drawer open more carefully? And as there isn't a single speck of dust, Ma must be dusting them in his absence, one by one.

In this drawer, other bodybuilding magazines and a photo with a dedication signed by Nagui* (a photo with a dedication signed by Nagui, Queequeg!). In another, spiral notebooks that I start to flick through. In them he jotted down with obsessive precision, to the nearest ounce and fraction of an inch, day in day out, his weight and his measurements, and his bodybuilding progress: neck, biceps, shoulders, chest, size measured at the sternum, waist measurement at the navel, thighs, calves. Insane lists of figures, some underlined in red. Number of sessions per week, exercises per session, repetitions per exercise . . . Weights lifted . . . Calculations of the amounts of proteins, fats and carbohydrates taken at each meal: so much chicken breast, so much low-fat cottage cheese, so much cereal with additives . . . vitamins, lecithin, leptin, carnitine, creatine, insulin, choline, ovalbumin and lactalbumin, amino acids . . . And then, I guess, the record of a more sinister bookkeeping: his dope, the junk he salted his soup with, to borrow Mr Luis's words: veterinary products, anabolic steroids, testosterone, and the like – the junk that killed him. Med, Sol, Dur, Bol, Clen, Glut: The names are mysteriously abbreviated and followed by a series of ten to twelve numbers – dates, amounts, and prices, I suppose.

– Damn, baby brother, you stink! And you see how you sweat?

* A well-known, Algerian-born French TV personality and comic

It was a white sweat, thick, greasy, frothy, like the foam on a horse's neck ... Sticky, yes, just like semen. And a smell of the butcher's, a funky smell of rotting dairy products. I also noticed that his skin had hardened and started to look like thick leather. But he just smiled inanely at me, to taunt me.

— Yeah, yeah, and when I piss in the dark, it's Pigalle! I piss neon, I shit orange. You should see it! Day-Glo shit! It's the boldone mixed with the clenbuterol that does that. They give it to horses, and I dope myself like a horse. I take a dose fit for a one-ton nag ... Yeah! One fix a week. Fucking right! With the IV, well, I'll spare you the details, but you know it's going to hurt! Your ass feels like concrete for a good hour, you can't move. But afterward it's great ... The first times, it's heaven: you lift the smallest dumbbell and – bang! – your biceps double in size ...

— And your liver gets two or three times as big! Mr Luis told me. And in the end your pancreas bursts. And your tendons snap ... They snap, Daniel! And your balls burst too! And you get cancer or Parkinson's like other people catch colds, Daniel! It's not true! You're crazy! You're not a horse, fuck it, you're not a horse!

But he neighs to rile me a bit more, and carries on:

— Nhhhin! Better than medol, better than durboline, better than soludecadron! To start with ...

— To start with ... Yeah! The first few times. But after that, then what?

— To start with, you feel all your muscles pumped full of blood, like having a hard-on all over ...

— All over except where it counts! Because as soon as you touch all that stuff, you can't get it up anymore. I know ...

— Mr Luis told me! He interrupts me, in a mocking, falsetto voice.

I make as if to hit him. I yell:

— You can't get it up anymore!

He answers quietly, bitter:

— No hard-ons or hard-ons for guys . . .

— Fuck it, I don't believe it! Baby bro! You're not going to bug me with that crap! I don't give a damn if you get fucked in the ass! I'm not Farid, I'm not Taouif! My kid brother can jack off with whoever he likes! I'd rather have you gay than dead. And if you carry on like this, you're going to kill yourself! Look! Your hands are shaking, fuck it! Just look at yourself in the mirror! It's not muscles anymore, it's just swelling! Pure beef! But shit, Daniel, you're not a piece of meat! You've got a soul! And where's your smarts in all this, hey!

— Anyway, I've always been stupid, so . . . It took me three tries to pass my exams, didn't it? And no good marks! I'll never find a decent job.

— Nor will I. That's not the point. There aren't any decent jobs for the likes of us – none at all. The Rumanians have got a better chance than us! . . . Anyway, you're no dumber than anyone else, and you know it. Fuck, you're no more stupid than me! Except when you shoot up anabolics, enough for a horse! Now, if it was real dope, so everything looked rosy, that I could understand. But it isn't! You're killing yourself for nothing, dammit!

— I don't give a fuck. I've had it. Anyhow, why should I go looking for a proper job? I can make twenty bucks in three hours at the peep show, half of it on the black!

As he spoke, he raised his chin, and had a defiant look, but his eyes were full of tears, and then he rested his forehead on my shoulder . . . And he started to sob.

— Don't cry on top of everything! Don't cry, baby bro!

The massive nape of his neck was running with foam, and the strong animal smell it emanated, more animal stench than sweat, made me feel a bit sick. Between two gulps he whispered:

— I'm full of hate, full of hate . . .

But he said it without any violence, almost without any hate. I wanted to tell him that the hate he felt was for himself, but words failed me.

My tears drip on to his spiral notebook, making the ink run and curling the squared paper, blurring the numbers he'd jotted down in it. His monstrous measurements ran together and were obliterated. I sling the notebook to the back of the drawer and push it closed again. The Goldoraks and the Darth Vaders that are still standing topple in turn. I'm suffocating. I'd like to stretch out on the bed – mine, his, I don't know any longer. And I don't know what stops me from doing so. Another memory encroaches, more remote but suddenly closer. I'm fourteen or fifteen. Daniel's eleven or twelve. He's grumbling about me being too fidgety at night before dropping off to sleep, shaking the bunk beds and waking him up when he's just fallen asleep.

The truth is that as soon as the light's out, I start to jerk off furiously into the patterned sheet, surrounded by waves, sails, compasses, compass roses, old parchments and treasures . . . I jerk off thinking about the blonds on the pontoon, last summer, or Mr Luis's accountant, another blond, primly dressed but with a bra that must be a 40 C, and I saw her the other day walking through the locker room without so much as an excuse me, as if it was all quite normal . . . As if she hadn't seen me!

Or, better still, Mrs Crémieux, the librarian. Annie. Annie! The tart, she asks me if I'd like to stay behind after school and give her a hand, help her to sort the books and organize the card index . . . If I'd like to! I've seen right through her game, the cunt: it's actually her who wants to lay little Smaïl! Just by chance she has to climb up the ladder to put some Conrads away. Fuck it, the bitch has got some ass! She asks me to pass her the books one by one . . . She's very polite, the bitch! That's their trick, bitches are all very polite! It's their way of saying you can get on with it, that's all they're waiting for! And, fuck it, she's not wearing panties! Annie's not wearing any panties! I'm right underneath her, I can see her bush! The prick tease, I'll be up that ladder and on her! Fuck her doggy-style! On the ladder! I hitch up her skirt, she doesn't say anything, she doesn't slap me. She wants it too badly, the bitch . . . She's wet, she moans like a bitch on heat! I spit into my hand to lubricate my dick . . . I . . . Ah!

— Shit! Stop it! Daniel snaps from up above. Stop moving about! You're making me seasick. I know what you're up to. I'll tell Dad!

— If you tell him, baby bro, I'll kill you! I swear!

— And first off, stop calling me baby bro! I'm fed up with it!

You had every reason to be fed up with it, baby bro: I was unbearable. But you didn't tell on me. You never let me down. The complicity between us was always really strong, the sense of honor. You covered up for me when I fucked up. I came to your defense when our father treated you like a moron and a lazy bum, screaming at you that you'd end up a hobo . . . Or that he really wanted a daughter rather than a son like you.

— *Er hat nicht geleiden* . . .

All of a sudden I didn't understand what the nurse said to me as she accompanied me to the elevator, but I thanked her:

— *Danke schön*.

Then, remembering the little German I know, I guessed she'd said what people always say in such circumstances: He hadn't suffered. But how would she know?

In an elevator 1, for me, means the first floor, so I pressed the next button down – U – and ended up in the *Untergeschoss*, the basement. The steel doors opened onto a view of piles of dirty laundry in trolleys, and a notice screwed to the far rough concrete wall pointing to *Desinfektion*.

In my confused state, I pushed 3, and went back up to the floor where my brother had just died . . . And then, by mistake again, I pushed U. The elevator went back down. But, thank God, the doors opened before it reached the basement, this time at the ground floor. And at last I got out of there fast.

There were telephones in the reception hall. I had to call Ma. Had to call Mama . . . To tell her about Daniel. To tell her.

If I reread on the screen what I've just written, things seem even more unreal. The words stand out too clearly against the lighted background to convey the vagueness, the trance-like state in which I lived through those moments of horror, splitting myself into two people. It's me and yet it's not altogether me who's doing what has to be done.

I could see myself doing things, I could see myself walking toward the elevator, and I could hear myself answering the nurse who told me my brother hadn't suffered: '*Danke schön.*' It was me, and then again it wasn't altogether me answering her. It was me pushing the U button by mistake in the elevator, and then again it wasn't altogether me. It was and wasn't me dialing 00 33 to call France, calling Ma . . . And me who carried on dialing another number: I'd get hold of my aunt Zaïa first. I just didn't have the courage to call Ma right away.

Then, the next day, still in a trance, I had to fill in forms and deal with Daniel's last wish – to be cremated. That his last hundredweight of anabolized muscles be reduced to ashes . . . A final punishment rather than a last wish, I said to myself. (I'm full of hate, full of hate, full of hate, full of hate – I could cut and paste *I'm full of hate* right down to the bottom of the page.) But I'll respect his wish.

The other thing that he left me was his gear.

* * *

Now I found myself in a modern, low-ceilinged office opposite a statutorily compassionate official – *sehr korrekt* – who handed me bundles of documents to sign. A secretary from the French consulate, who was every bit as administratively humane, sensitive and courteous, translated the few lines above the dotted line where I had to sign my name. I had a choice of procedures: either repatriate the body or have it cremated here in Germany and take the urn back to France, free of charge.

— You're, er . . . French?

— French, yes. Born in France, French father.

A grandfather who died for France, an uncle murdered by the French police on Papon's orders . . . I didn't add.

She told me my rights and what the law said: green EEC label, free movement of goods . . . (Goods, Daniel!)

The day after next, at Hamburg Airport, a security person stuck a red adhesive strip on the urn marked IDENTIFIED PARCEL. But the alarm went off when I walked through the metal detector.

— *Was ist das*?

— My brother's ashes.

— *Was?*

— Ashes . . . My brother.

I didn't have any anger left in me, or sorrow. It was and wasn't me walking through the metal detector.

I pick up the urn that I'd put on the bed. I've got to rush, it's my shift at Speedzza. But what shall I do with it? I can't deliver pizzas with . . .

The cupboard. Pushing one of the sliding doors. I see that my brother didn't try to extend his territory once I'd left home, which would have been quite normal. On the right, the hangers and shelves were still empty. (It was all yours, Daniel.)

He never got into cross country, or motor-biking, for that matter. The only bike he ever drove in his life, like me, was the red moped for delivering pizzas – the fucking shame of it! But he liked cross-country gear: the padded pants, the big belt, the elbow-pads, the chest protector, the heavy boots – *Tuareg*-style. In the catalog, bikers pose with the Sahara as a backdrop . . . A coat of armour that would have protected him, but from what? For delivering pizzas he had to make do with the red oilskin uniform, the light helmet, and boots – Speedzza doesn't allow any fancy stuff. Me too, I'll make do with wearing his boots, which he insisted on bequeathing to me, God only knows why.

His treasures, his secrets are locked away in a silver metal chest with wrought-iron fittings, Moroccan crafts-manship, that Zaïa, I think it was, gave him. Did he ever realize I'd finally sussed out the lock combination: 5317? I turn the rings – 5, 3, 1, 7 – and hear the click. The padlock opens.

Daniel's treasures, his secrets? Postcards and greeting cards sent by classmates, beautiful white pebbles from the beach, some dirhams, two crisp new 500-franc bills, an Ironman watch with a broken dial, a letter several pages long in its envelope, postmarked in Germany – which I forbid myself to read, though I badly wanted to. Accessories for the peep show: a studded chest harness, a gold satin G-string, and a huge dildo to slip inside it, and the black rubber mask. Two tiny holes for the eyes and two for the nostrils . . . I was curious to try it on, but I didn't know how to put it on right. The cold, airtight material pressed over my nose, the more I inhaled the more I suffocated in the dark. It's as if I'd put a cap-of-death on. Anxiety got the better of me, I panicked, and took it off so fast that it tore . . . After that I had trouble getting my breath back.

In the chest of drawers I also found some sheets of coarse-grained, cream-colored drawing paper. I'd forgotten what fun I used to have when I was fourteen, fifteen. I'd draw maps of our treasure islands with a felt-tip, then I'd roll them up like parchment when I'd blackened the edges with the flame of a candle . . . And classy serrated paper that I wrote on for him, in my decorative hand, with gold-flecked black ink – Arab proverbs, lines of verse, birthday wishes . . . Or these words of Rimbaud: *Moi, je suis intact, et ça m'est égal* – I'm intact, and it's all the same to me.

I put the urn away at the back of the cupboard, locked the chest again, and called Zaïa to ask her to come and keep Ma company. Ma was still sitting there, on a stool, rocking gently back and forth. I told her I'd be back when I'd done my Speedzza shift. She just nodded: Go along, my son . . . I didn't kiss her, I was too afraid she might suddenly cling to me and delay me. If the truth be told, I could have cried off, they hadn't seen me around for twelve days at Speedzza, so what was one more day . . .? But I couldn't stand that tearless, choked grief. And I felt it would probably give me some relief for a moment, to howl through the city on the moped and deliver a few pizzas, blow off some steam in the thick of the traffic, slap a bit of pizza dough around and stir the topping mix, like vomit, see people who wouldn't be in mourning, people waiting at home for their special-offer ham-'n'-anchovy maxi-Regina while they watched the evening news on TV, with the usual anchorman.

When I got to the lab – they call it the lab at Speedzza – when I walked through the door, not a soul asked me anything about Daniel. Taouif didn't, Gamal didn't, nor did Bruno or Mickey or Pinocchio, even though I'd told them all why I had to go to Hamburg . . . *Oualou*, nothing, zilch. Not a word. Hardly a 'Hey, man! How's it going?' and a high five . . . OK. I clock in, slip on a pair of shiny red pants over my trousers . . . Back to it! Get rid of my thoughts. Above all, don't dwell on Daniel, who worked here ... At Speedzza we were one big happy family, so-called: 'a mini-structure, five franchises in Paris, seven in the 'burbs, superhot service, supercool attitude' – I'm quoting the boss, Mr Beni. Whereas at Pizza Shit-house, as we nickname our number-one competitor, the fat multinational, it's a sweatshop by all accounts. And when it comes to getting a job there, you might as well be applying for a senior management vacancy at IBM! Preliminary interviews, assessment tests, cross-examination, and then more cross-examination ... Your police record, your last three school report books, your parents' and your grandparents' first names, their nationality ... Your sexual orientation ... Have you ever suffered from depression? Mental disorders? Have you been a boy scout? A party activist? Which party? A member of a club? Which one? Do you have team spirit? And a sense of sacrifice? Would you be more motivated by the prospect of personal success or the success of the company employing you? How many toothbrushes do you get through in a year? Do you use a deodorant every day? Do you wash your hands before you go to the lavatory? Always – often – sometimes – never? Do you wash your hands after you've been to the lavatory? Always – often – sometimes – never? In not more than thirty words say what fascinates you about pizzas and about home delivery. What other product might interest you? Do you speak fluent English (answer this question in English)? Fill in the figures, tick boxes, delete where not applicable, write legibly.

I can see my brother again, coming back from the cross-examination totally wasted. Once again he'd been turned down for a job. He'd flunked the very last test, which consisted of drawing a line through the word that didn't belong in the list. Example: One of the following ingredients is not part of the recipe for our famous all-American pizzzzzas: flour – salt – love – tomato – margarine – which? Daniel had crossed out the word 'love,' but he should have crossed out 'margarine.' There's plenty of love in their pizzas, but there's no margarine.

Despair, anger, indignation. He said mechanically, over and over:

— I'm a jerk, I'm a jerk, I'm a jerk . . .

I was even more up in arms than he was.

— Fuck it, d'you need an MBA from Harvard, these days, to deliver pizzas?

But there was no call for surprise, because it's become the rule, because it's all worked out and planned. That's how it's set up – everywhere. Because these continual humiliations, that we're subjected to when we go looking for work, any kind of work, are not caused by negligence or indifference, which would already be shocking enough. No, they're the result of a conscious plan on the part of the haves to get rid of that human resource, the working man! They do everything they possibly can to upset us, put us down, break our spirits and make us crazy – a little bit of love in every all-American pizzzza! Toeing the line, selection process, psychological torture, apprenticeship through fear tactics, schooling in bondage, brainwashing, elimination . . . Eliminating a whole generation of young men, just like in the 1914–18 war. This is a war, too. Oh no! They're not sending us to our death in the trenches of Verdun, no; instead, they're killing us with shame and boredom. We're dole-fodder the way those others were cannon-fodder . . . And all those CVs sent off in their hundreds – for nothing! And the job interviews – for nothing! And the unsolicited job applications – for nothing! *Oualou*. No way. And worse still the training courses: the lies, the legal fiddling, the travesty of work, at any cost . . . *Oualou-ou-ou-ou-ou-ou*! No way, no way, no way! Job-welfare contracts, job-initiative contracts, consolidated job contracts after a job-welfare contract, alternate qualification contracts, alternate job adaptation contracts, business access courses, job integration and training courses . . . What more? Clowns! Crooks! Fascists! In Arabic we say *oualou*, meaning: nothing. Hot air.

Beside himself with anger, Daniel kicked the wall with his metal boot tips, yelling:

– I've had it! Up to here! I'm gonna shoot myself, I'm gonna . . . Wait, no, I'll do it like a Human Bomb: sticks of dynamite in my belt, but fuck it, I won't let those fuckers from the swat squad hunt me down, I'll blow everything to bits first, motherfucker! And not some high-class daycare center in Neuilly . . . I'll go straight for the President in his Elysée Palace, that's what I'll do!

– Cut the crap, baby brother, cut the crap! Calm down now.

– Fucking hell, the dickheads! Flour, salt, love, tomato, margarine!

There's no margarine in the famous Speedzza pizza recipe either. If only! On the oil cans there's no mention of oil, just: *hot-emulsified compound fat – 'olive' flavouring* (*olive* in inverted commas). The herbs and spices are synthetic, the pepper's in a spray can. The cheese comes in five-pound rubbery white bricks, wrapped in heat-sealed plastic. The crab is made from fish waste with E104 colorant – produce of Madagascar. And when the boss has forgotten to rip off the label, you can still read on the cans of boned ham: *Re-importation into an EEC member country is strictly prohibited and punishable by law*.

Mr Beni's wheeling and dealing. Like Péquod, he pulls out all the stops when it comes to government measures, makes the most of the slightest tax break, and the slightest exemption from social security contributions. He pays us badly, half under the table, doesn't make 'a penny profit' – he tells us – and 'only pays himself a thousand a month' – he tells us – and drives a Porsche and plays golf at Marbella – which is what he doesn't tell us. But he also told us he supported Chirac because it was important to 'cut down the social bill' – and he said bill, not ill.

There's no margarine, but there's no love, either, in Speedzza pizzas. The team gets its own back as best it can: We've got our own private lingo, pizza-ese, which tells how we feel about it all. We call the frozen dough that's delivered every other day from the main depot the

52

fudge. When the dough's ready for the oven, it's the *doughnut*. The garnish is known as *vomit*. Peeled tomatoes, the *runs*. The cheese, *jism*. Ham, *ass*.

— Motherfucker! I told you no ass, the guy's a Yid!

— Why didn't he order the Napoli, stupid fuck!

— Pass me the runs, fuck it, the runs, Mickey, I'm short!

— Whoa, you there! You've put too much jism on it. You're ruining it!

— The slag! She's really thinking about it! She wants a bit of anchovy added!

— On the special? And my dick, it's cool too?

— What shall I tell her?

— It's the vomit of the day or the full price, fuck it, so don't be a pain in the ass!

— Sorry, Madam, the manager says we can't add anything extra to the special of the day. Sorry.

— I know that slut, too, lives on Avenue Junot! She's not in a hurry to tip you, fucking whore! Its ninety-eight francs, motherfucker, and she hands you a hundred-franc note and waits for her two francs change, the slut! And two door-codes and all, and an intercom, and a kind of sixth-floor courtyard opposite, staircase B kind of place, with a huge fucking mutt that barks at you, fuck it . . . A smidgen of anchovy!

The customer who's a pain in the ass, the customer on the phone who takes ten minutes to decide between the Baltic and the Oriental, the guy who wants to know if the merguez sausage is really Beth Din-certified kosher, the woman who orders a Regina for two, no mushrooms but extra artichoke – five francs – and the artichokes on just one side of the pizza, please, and no herbs on the other side, please, and a couple of beers, one Kronenbourg, ice-cold in a bottle if you've got it, and the other, yes, a Corona, room temperature, OK? Pinocchio adds – free of charge – a special condiment before sliding the pizza into the oven, the pizza-chef's special touch: a big gob of spit or some snot. (I'm telling you this, dear reader, in case you still felt like ordering a Speedzza pizza!)

– And one Regina with extra artichokes to go!

Pinocchio and Gamal take it in turns at the oven. But Mr Beni makes sure the switchboard operator and the delivery boys all help with the dough, between three and seven of us, depending on the day and the time. The dough has to be kneaded as it unfreezes – we call it 'slapping the fudge.' And then the topping . . . And we have to get the drinks and little containers of ice cream out of the freezer . . . and fill the boxes . . . And slip them into the thermal packs . . . And stack them in the top case, the 'canteen'. And check the route on the map . . . Not forgetting the slip of paper with the address and code . . . Get your jacket on . . . and your helmet . . . and Go!

Then comes the only heady part of the job, when you get to feel a bit high: grab the handles, gun the back wheel, and with all your senses at the ready hurl yourself into the fray, zigzag, take aim and roll, burn rubber, shoot the lights, to hell with one-way signs, screech on the pavement, keep an eye out for the cops, get your ass out of there fast when they whistle – watch out for car doors, scream at anything that moves and, even more so, at anything that isn't moving:

– Move, motherfucker, asshole! Make room, *halouf*, pig, bastard, down there, shit! Move it! Motherfucker! Move it! The red light's green!

A kick of the heel at old heaps that won't get out of the way, cutting in front of the moped boys from Pizza Shithouse ... Rush of adrenaline ... Shrieks like wild beasts hunting ... High on stress ... Amok! I'm not Paul Smaïl anymore, with an MA in comparative literature under the supervision of Mrs. Danièle Casenave, Paris University – *Herman Melville in France: translations, publications and criticism* – I'm a Speedzza delivery boy, and I'd kill to save thirty seconds on a delivery.

Park fast and lock, quickly get the thermal containers out, punch in the code, leap up the stairs, and ring the bell ... But who's going to open? An OK customer or some crazy?

People don't necessarily order a pizza because they want a pizza, but rather for the fantasy of it, or to comfort themselves, or for the social contact, as those psycho-socio-whatchacallits say in that drivel you hear on TV. Beware when the order's for just one pizza and just one drink: could be a woman just given the shove, missing her guy perhaps. Or some lonesome faggot. What he really wanted was a Napoli with a side order of company – fifty francs. One night an old queen asked me if I'd give him a quickie blowjob on my knees, still in my helmet, with my gloves on. 'No thanks. At Speedzza we only do pizzas! If you want a blowjob, check with Pizza Shithouse. Their number's in the book ...' But I'm making it up. I didn't answer that tight-ass. I left without saying a word, as if I hadn't heard, slamming the door quite hard behind me, that's all. (A question for Daniel: 'And would you have done it for five hundred francs? And for five thousand?')

In winter they see you coming up frozen, your cheeks

all raw, and they ask if you want to get warm. In summer, you're pickled in the oilskin, you stink, and that's what excites them even more.

There are some who open their door wearing a dressing gown, their hair wet, and, as if by accident, the belt of the dressing gown comes undone just when they're taking the pizza box from you. Or alternatively they've left their wallet in the bedroom: if you feel like following them . . .!

There are some people – mainly women – who say, when they're placing the order, that they only want Bruno to deliver it. Either because he's got fair hair and blue eyes – so therefore he's not an A-rab – or because he's got fair hair and blue eyes – so he's very cute – or because he's not threatening – but I'm saying all this without really knowing. If it's Gamal or Taouif taking the order, they invariably say their colleague isn't available. If it's me, I don't give a damn: I send them Bruno.

But you also get a group of friends who're already smashed on pastis or Kronenbourg when you ring at the door, and they get their kicks pulling your leg – they'll ask you if you're the plumber, they'll hide your helmet, say there's one pizza too many, to be taken back, and then they split the bill ten ways, and it takes forever to get all the money, or else they get involved with endless picky calculations, making sure that everyone pays only what he owes: 'Mine's an Atlantic, half a bottle of rosé, and a brownie . . . That's ninety . . . Yours is a Baltic, half a bottle of rosé, and a brownie . . . that's ninety-five . . .! Five francs more, check the list!' That's when they're not breaking into the kids' piggybanks to count out two hundred and twenty one-franc pieces! That's happened to me too.

It was a karaoke night, and a moron, naked to the waist, was bawling a song into the mike: 'Is this how people live?'

Yeah. There are also customers who never have the exact change but never want to leave you a little extra. There are those who forget to sign the check, and if you only realize it afterward you go back and ring the doorbell: *Keutchi* Zilch! – they won't open up. Then there are those who ordered just the one Napoli solo, and they're five round the table, and they ask for a pile of paper napkins and end up begrudgingly giving you a twenty-cent tip with a sigh. And those who've kept you hanging about for a quarter of an hour and more before opening the door because they're in the middle of the soap on TV, and then they go and call the shop to complain that their Oriental is lukewarm. Every time. Every time.

But the worst thing for the delivery boy is those evenings when there's a big match. It's fine driving through the deserted streets, but when he gets to the door, heaven help him if he rings in the middle of a crucial attack, or just after the ref's whistled a penalty! It's often better to wait for halftime before you unpack the goods and collect the money. One time, Daniel got the steaming-hot Maxi Four Cheese he was delivering SMACK in the face – it was some Marseilles supporters who were so plastered they'd forgotten their own names: Bavaria Dortmund was leading two–nil! There's not a single guy at Speedzza who can't tell some equally heavy Cup night story for which he's paid the price.

Then you get your fascists, who ask you if you've got a

valid residence permit, or if you're an illegal immigrant, or if you're really French. And you get your paranoids, who refuse to give you their code and pace up and down outside the doorway of their building until you turn up. Or people who give you the code so you can get into the building but then ask you, from behind their closed door, to put the pizza boxes on the doormat, watching your every move through the peephole, and slide their check under the door, and then wait till you're in the elevator and have pushed the button before they furtively open the door and take their order.

— America's the place! Mr Beni sniggers, still very proud to let you know he's lived over there. 'No payroll taxes and no minimum wage! Total freedom! You can fire an employee in two minutes with a kick in the butt! You pay people what you feel like, at the going rate! The guy who wants to work, he works! And if he works, he eats! Otherwise, you throw the bum out! No sitting around over there! Because you'll be fired: just like that! And there's no obligatory Social Security payments either! Chirac ought to do the same here. People here are too pampered – too insisted. That's the price of molly-coddling . . .'

(You don't say! We're too insisted. That's where the welfare bill comes from.)

But I'd be unfair if I didn't add that you can also meet decent customers, who think of us as their neighbors, not their slaves, who smile at us and say hello, thanks and even: 'That was quick.' Or, if we arrive soaked and dripping: 'Poor thing! What a downpour!' And leave a ten or twelve percent tip, and don't slam the door as soon as your back's turned but push it quietly to.

The slightest act of human kindness can move us deeply. We talk about it back at the shop, by the ovens, and we forget all our filthy language:

— The kid stuck his tongue out at me, but his mother said: 'Say you're sorry. If this man hadn't come, you wouldn't have anything to eat tonight . . .'

— You serious?

But you can't get emotional because you've got to move on:

For the Comédie de Paris, Rue Fontaine, two Baltics, two Four Cheese, one Bermuda with a double topping of cheese, one Oriental, one Napoli, one Calzone, plus: one Red, one Evian, three Kros, three Coronas, three chocolate chip ice creams, one strawberry-vanilla, one brownie, two bikes, Mickey and Paul, *r'ajoulaïn* . . . step on it . . .

— *Labès*. That's cool.

Bent over the scooter, cleaving the air, in your mind's eye you're out at sea, on an adventure, sailing into the wind, beating close to windward, heave ho, hoist the royal, all sails . . . And sails flapping . . . Albatrosses in the wake . . . Salt on the lips . . . Sun in the eyes . . . *Free man, you will always cherish the sea! I hail you, old ocean! It is refound! – what? – Eternity! Azure! azure! azure! azure! But when, my brother, shall we see the green shore of the Promised Land?*

— Green! Go on! Move, you lump of shit! Move it! Get your lousy wreck moving! Step on it! And my finger, you stupid jerk, my finger, where d'you want it?

The lady who'd ordered a Vegetariana with extra onion-pepper-broccoli topping – ten francs more – and a cheap bottle of red – ninety-eight francs total – asked me if I could help her mend the door of her dishwasher, which had just fallen off. She wasn't going to call the dealer for something so trivial. If I'd just like to hold the door for her while she screwed the hinges back on . . .

– But of course, madam! Or the other way round: you hold the door for me while I screw it back on. I've probably got a stronger grip than you.

– Wipe your feet well! And, wait! I'll give you a floor-cloth. Is it raining outside?

– Outside, madam, yes, inside, no, aren't we lucky!

She pursed her lips with annoyance and ushered me in, but as if against her better judgment. Three of the walls of her studio apartment were lined with books, floor to ceiling; there were even books in the kitchen. I gasped, as if someone had just punched me straight in the stomach:

– Wow! So many books!

A copy of *Moby Dick* was wedged between the salt-cellar and a tea caddy. To show off, while I tightened the screws, I said, all innocent like:

– Ah, in the translation by Giono, Lucien Jacques and Joan Smith . . . *Je m'appelle Ishmael. Mettons . . .*

Dynamite: Mrs Moriot looked me up and down, mouth wide open and inquired as to what I did in life, apart

60

from delivering pizzas for Speedzza. She'd heard that delivery boys were often students, but this was the first time . . . Truly, she'd never have thought that someone with a knowledge of literature . . . And if I liked reading as much as I said I did, she had a job to offer me: She ran a bookstore and she was looking for a part-time assistant, Wednesday evenings, all day Saturday and Sunday mornings.

– It would definitely be more rewarding for you, intellectually, than delivering pizzas . . .

(Paul Smaïl, to Paul Smaïl: What does she know about it?)

She handed me her bookstore card, 'Les Livres sur la Butte.' She said I should call her the following day at lunchtime. For her it was a done deal. And because she was offering me a job, she felt exempt from having to give me a tip as well, despite the helping hand I'd given her with her dishwasher – she had the exact change, ninety-eight francs, on the nose.

In any case she was left wing, so she didn't agree with tipping. Tips are a demeaning practice that perpetuates class divisions and distorts social relationships. This was also why she no longer filled in her payslips the way she should, or complied with the law obliging the employer to pay people double time on Sundays. We shouldn't regard her as our boss, but rather as our friend. And after all, if we weren't Christians, then Sunday for us was just another day like all the rest, wasn't it? She wasn't a religious person, she was a nonconformist, so paying double time on Sundays was like giving in to some ridiculous superstition. Wasn't working in a bookstore rewarding enough? Didn't we all form a community bonded together by our worship of books? A bookstore isn't an ordinary business. Working in a bookstore isn't a trade, it's a mission! Either you have a love of literature in your blood or you don't! And to think that she'd had employees who'd been petty-minded enough to haul her up in front of the labor relations board! That was because they didn't have the calling.

With her little round metal-framed glasses, her pudding-bowl haircut, not a trace of makeup, not a jewel in sight, her white blouse buttoned to the neck and a scout-mistress's dark-blue pleated skirt, Mrs Moriot did indeed look every bit the missionary. In the Salvation Army, or a Rumanian Communist Youth activist Rumania under Ceauşescu . . . The day she took me on, I learned that the people working for her nicknamed her the Abbess.

'Les Livres de la Butte' – 'Books on the Hill' – looked just like its owner: monastically austere, white wood and rough stone, not a flower or poster anywhere – nothing excessive. Mrs Moriot removed the strips and dust jackets from her books, and railed against four colour covers. She'd have ripped them right off if she could have. And she swore by the Editions de Minuit, nobody else:

– They're serious people. Not ostentatious.

She introduced me to my fellow employees – Myriam, Laurent, and Fabrice:

– I'm so pleased somebody from North Africa is joining us. For our bookstore this means an opening out to the world . . .

Myriam flashed me an apologetic glance and smiled at me, as if she wanted to say she was sorry about her boss's tactlessness. Laurent pulled a face on the sly, and looked like he was thinking: Really, she never misses a chance!

As for Fabrice, I hadn't been there ten minutes before he managed to whisper into my ear, looking for all the world as if he wasn't up to anything, without so much as parting his teeth:

— Four months! Nobody has ever stuck it out here more than four months. Just thought I'd warn you. I've been here since September 15th and I know I'll be fired at the first opportunity, right after the post-Christmas sales, I'll bet. With her it always ends up at a labor relations board. She loses every time, but she doesn't care. She's a fascist. She thinks she's left wing because she goes to all the demos, but she's a fascist. And if there weren't three million unemployed people, she wouldn't find anyone to work for her.

You could almost touch not only the contempt that all three felt for her, but also the vague terror she inspired in them. It all made the air hard to breathe. By comparison, the atmosphere at Speedzza seemed quite calm when I reported there in the evening.

But if I felt disappointed, I had only myself to blame. Because, right away, I should have guessed what to expect. I hadn't liked the shrill tone of her voice when she'd said: 'For you it would definitely be more fulfilling, intellectually, than delivering pizzas . . .' Unfortunately, I didn't go with my instincts.

The Abbess's unctuous clear conscience! Her motherliness! The two-faced, nervous kind of way she spoke to her friend from North Africa . . . The way some colonial wife would have spoken to the darkie pruning her roses.

— Paul, this gentleman would like a paperback copy of *The Idiot*. Could you find it for him?

— Yes, ma'am, under D in Russian literature.

— Good. And if I asked you for *Le Grand Meaulnes*, Paul?

Under A – French fiction, ma'am. Alain-Fournier. We don't put him under the Fs. Alain wasn't his first name. (Right.)

— Good. Good. But, Paul dear, why don't you call me Jehanne . . .

No way. Paul dear . . . whatever next? Keep your distance, my friend! Arm's length, as Mr Luis would say. Given the changes she made to the standard contract of employment, and the rambling spiel she gave to excuse them, don't get familiar with the Abbess! All-out war! *Jihad*! Mr Beni himself, king of rip-offs, doesn't march along behind the 'Movement against Anti-Semitism' and the 'League against Racism' banners, but he treats his slaves better . . . Or let's say not quite as badly.

No, I hadn't followed my instincts: That old maid dressed up like a nun, ordering a Vegetariana, had the exact change, and wore metal-rimmed glasses! But . . . those books! All those books! That's what I thought of before anything else. I was exhilarated. I was over-excited, the way I am whenever I walk into a bookstore or a library. Or when I pay a visit to Mr Hamel, my old French teacher, who must have at least several thousand books . . . Except that in Mr Hamel's house I don't dare touch them, or open them, or leaf through them. And in the library you have to consult the card index and be content with just two or three titles at a time, no more. Whereas there, I was like a little kid who hears the man in the toyshop say to him: 'Take anything you want!'

I didn't hold back. I'd take a novel from a table or shelf, open it at random, flick through it, read the opening lines, and peruse a page or two . . . Then I'd put it back, take another one that looked more interesting, hide behind a pillar to read in peace, forgetting straightaway that I was there to sell books, not to read them. Mrs. Moriot would call out:

— Paul!

— Just a sec . . .

— Paul, there's nobody at the cash register . . .

— Just a sec, I said . . .

— Paul, but Paul, what are you up to?

— I'm reading, ma'am . . .

Myriam, alarmed, struck dumb and all aquiver on my behalf, urged me with her big dark eyes to run over and apologize. Laurent and Fabrice were sniggering behind their hands, taking my foolhardiness for uppitiness, something they'd never have dreamed of doing. They looked at me as if I were a desperado about to leap into the middle of Les Livres de la Butte with his bomb – window in smithereens, ceiling collapsing, pillars tottering . . . But no. All unctuous, with endless patience and understanding, Mrs Moriot proceeded to explain to her nice little raghead that it was a good thing to read, but, please, out of friendship for her, please not during working hours.

— Come here, Paul, I want to show you how to fill in the green cards for restocking.

As I turned down the corner of the page, I heard myself mumble, in English:

— I'd rather not.

— What was that?

I repeated Bartleby's answer in Melville's novel: *I'd rather not*.

But why this suicidal behavior? Because I knew I was heading for a fall, I knew that the next thing I did, or the one after, would be the end. One fight too many, as boxers say. I was on trial: One more word and the Abbess would get rid of the dirty A-rab who didn't want to go along with the rules she'd made for her staff. She'd get rid of him with a degree of brutality that matched the kindness with which she'd taken him in and encouraged him to improve himself intellectually . . . A pizza boy! Really, these Arabs! Beyond the pale! So arrogant! And so lazy!

No illusions. I could imagine my firing, I could hear myself screaming blue murder at her, offloading everything weighing on my heart, all onto her. I was enjoying it ahead of time. It was as if I'd undergone years of fear and humiliation working for her, and was finally getting my own back. Whereas I'd been working at La Butte for only three weeks, not even, and for just sixteen hours a week.

I shouldn't have riled her like that, I knew as much, but I couldn't help myself. It was stronger than me. The need, I guess, to assert myself, even if it made me look like a lunatic. Some childish desire, but irresistible, to play the big shot to impress my colleagues. Myriam, above all.

And yet I really wasn't in love with Myriam. No. Really not. Besides, love at first sight doesn't exist in the real world. It's a novelist's invention – some lousy, schmaltzy novelist. And then Myriam wasn't really my type. No. Because I liked only blonds with blue eyes, big tits and little noses, real blonds with fair skin, shiksas, the way you fantasize about them when you come from an Arab neighborhood . . . or the Barbès, where all the North

Africans live. No, I couldn't fall in love with Myriam.
Myriam was very brown, with an olive complexion, big
dark eyes, small breasts, and a nose . . . *Hafif*, Paul!

But if I stopped reading for a split second, it was to
check her out, have a look at her without her knowing –
her big dark eyes, her smile at once ironical and shy, her
long neck, her delicate hands, her gentle voice, the way
she tucked her cheek into the hollow of her shoulder, the
way she lifted her mass of long dark hair over her ear,
only to have it then tumble softly down again . . . In the
end, between Nabokov and Myriam, Myriam won the
day: I closed *Pale Fire*, put the book back in the display
stand, and walked over to her.

— Need a hand, miss?

— You can call me Myriam, Paul.

— If you like.

A customer was looking for a novel he'd heard about
the night before on TV. He couldn't remember what
program, in fact it might have been a couple of nights
ago, or it could have been on the radio. He'd forgotten
the author's name and the exact title. All he could
remember was that the title had the word *heart* in it, he
was sure about that.

— *The Heart-Snatcher*?

— No.

— *The Heart Trap*?

— No.

— *The Heart is a Lonely Hunter*?

— No, no. It's on the tip of my tongue. It's a story about
sailors.

— *Heart of Darkness*.

— That's it!

Giggles only just stifled, knowing winks between Myriam and me. But how come I'm so touched all of a sudden?

When the customer had left, she whispered to me, making sure Mrs Moriot couldn't hear:

— And it's like that all day long! Yesterday, a woman wanted a Victor Hugo novel for her godson. It took place in Spain, the story of some mad knight . . .

— *Don Quixote*?

— Wrong! *Monte Cristo*.

— I'll never stick it. I give up. And what with the boss . . .

— No, please! Don't quit! Make an effort!

It was a plea from the heart, from someone who'd taken me into her confidence so readily, and Myriam blushed all over. But as for me – *hrala*, shit – instead of feeling on top of the world, instead of trying to please her by making an effort, I then actually made things worse. Ah, how impenetrable things are! I became even more aggressive with Mrs Moriot. And with customers I cultivated a coldness bordering on discourtesy. Weird way of trying to seduce someone!

The fact was, though, that I couldn't shake off a feeling of powerlessness. I'd never know how to go about escorting Myriam to the subway, after work, as if it were the most normal thing to do. I never dared offer her a coffee. I never dared tell her that . . . that what?

I was helpless. I found myself ugly, and terribly awkward. I told myself that if she happened to find out that I was a boxer, she'd reckon I was dodgy and not her type at all. Too much of a lout for her, not sophisticated enough. It didn't help if I went via Rue Ordener to have a bath before turning up at the bookstore on Saturdays and Sunday mornings. It wasn't any good my lathering up and showering longer than usual, on Wednesdays, after my session with Mr Luis. I always had the feeling that I stank, that I was impregnated with all the sweat in the gym and all the grub at Speedzza. I smelled like a Barbès Arab. I was a poor wog, and Myriam Fink was a Jewish princess.

And then the last straw: The Abbess said to her:

— Do you know how I found Paul, Myriam? I'd ordered a pizza, and he was the one who delivered it. And he was kind enough to mend the door of my dishwasher . . .

I could have killed her, killed her, killed her . . . I will kill her. The knife we use to split open the boxes of books . . . That's it. The knife! The *beur*'s weapon! Take up the cutter! Stabbed by the Moroccan! Go straight for the jugular – *hra*!

She hands me a book by Driss Chraïbi. *Past Historic*. And another by Mohamed Choukri, *Plain Bread*.

— Here! she says to me, these should interest you.

I don't answer. I don't tell her I've read them both already. I blurt out:

— Oh really? And why's that?

Disconcerted, she beats a hasty retreat. Anyway, she's got to go: Saturdays, at lunchtime, she leaves the store in our hands for a couple of hours while she goes to her transcendental yoga class.

— I'm off. Be good!

Straightaway the staff cheers up. It's a bit like at school, when the recreation bell rings. Laurent whistles, Fabrice jokes with the regular customers leafing through new titles. I suddenly feel full of enthusiasm. And I'm not in the least bit intimidated by the customers anymore. I tell a kid asking me for *The Little Prince*:

— No, hold on! How much have you got? Fifty francs? Mind if I recommend something else? *The Little Prince* is pretty stupid. Have you read *Treasure Island*? I'd take *Treasure Island* instead if I were you.

To a guy I've seen parking his BMW outside the store, and who is losing it because a five-hundred-page novel costs a hundred and twenty-nine francs, I say:

— If you don't mind me asking, sir, how much did your car cost you?

And to a woman who's taken aback because she can't find the latest book by Nadine de Rothschild, I say:

— This is a bookstore, madam. You'll find toilets at the Funicular.

Laurent turns away toward a pillar so he can laugh more comfortably. Fabrice, however, issues a warning:

— You'd better watch it! Don't be so rude to people! There are some who might well come in later and rat on you to the boss.

Myriam gives him an approving look.

I raise my hands skyward, fatalistically: Let them come and tell tales! *Hamdou l'lah*!

But we didn't notice the time passing. We're all there laughing like drains at some joke told us by an old local eccentric who spends his days reading at Les Livres de la Butte, when the Abbess pushes the door open. Transcendental yoga apparently did not bring her serenity:

— What's all this? she shrieks aggressively. Looks like everyone's messing about when I'm not here! And meanwhile there's the Hachette package that's been waiting around for two days, at least two days! And you still haven't opened it!

She grabs the cutter, furiously impales the adhesive tape around the box. The blade squeaks and rips the covers of the topmost books. She hands one to me: Rachid Mimouni's *The Curse*.

— For you, Paul.

Beside myself, I shout back:

— Because he's a raghead, too, huh? Because he's a sand-nigger? I've had an assful of your crass remarks, bitch! Dammit, you're a pain in the butt! And d'you want to know why, huh? A-rabs should only read books by A-rabs, is that what you think? Then Proust is just for faggots, is that right? And Melville too? And Virginia Woolf's just for dykes? And what about Bretons? They should just read Chateaubriand? Russians, Tolstoy? But not Dickens, huh, Dickens is for the English! He was English, Dickens. A raghead can't read Dickens! Is that what you want then? Each to his own! Serbs with Serbs, Croats with Croats, and the rest behind barbed wire! What the fuck have I got to do with Arab literature? For me, there are good books and bad books, period. But you, for two seconds you can't forget I come from ... You're obsessed by it! But I'm French, get it! Like you. No more, no less. French by birth, if you want to know. You want to see my papers? The only difference between us, the only difference is that the cops ask to see my papers more often than they ask you! *The Curse*! No, fuck it, I don't believe it! *The Curse*! Stupid bitch! Our curse is people like you. It's people like you who give us Le Pen! It's not so much the nasty little suburban fascists, it's people like you, antiracists and all, so-called. Stupid cunts like you ... Fuck you! Fuck you! I'm outta here! Serious professional misconduct: I called the boss a stupid cunt!

Repeat: a stupid cunt! Ah! And you can strip-search me too if you want. I haven't been in the cash register. I should have: Ragheads steal from the cash register, we all know that! Wogs steal from the cash register and at night, before they go to sleep, they read Mimouni! *The Curse*! They improve themselves, intellectually.

Holding the knife, the Abbess was lost for words. She seemed paralyzed. Laurent and Fabrice didn't say anything either, not daring to butt in. Myriam was on the verge of tears. As for the customers, they'd all made a dash for the door – one of them making the most of the moment to shoplift a book: the detector beeped.

As calmly as I could, I walked through the bookstore, and took my backpack and jacket from the storeroom. As I passed, I knocked over a pile of books, but I swear it wasn't on purpose. What's more, I picked them up.

As I left, I made a thing of pulling down the zip of my bag and opened it wide to show my ex-boss, as if she'd accused me of shoplifting . . . she looked uneasy! A satisfying uneasiness – for me.

And outside, to a few inquisitive customers who'd witnessed the rest of the scene through the window, I said, amiably:

— You can go back in. It's over.

End of my brief experience in a bookstore.

Myriam.

I wrote her name at the top of a page in my notebook and instantly turned the page. Impossible to go on. Fear. What's called refusing to fight, if writing's a form of combat. But doesn't fighting come into it a bit? Every boxer will tell you that the hardest thing, in boxing, is to have a rematch with an opponent who beat you last time around. Getting into the ring without being overcome by painful memories of all the punches you took, or memories of painful punches, without reliving your defeat or wanting to make up for it ... without an ounce of resentment. Brand-new, in a word. Untouched. Innocent.

But how can I tell you what our love was like without rekindling feelings, without once again painfully raising all the questions that were asked, without suffering too much while recalling that lost happiness now that everything's over between us? Now that everything's over but nothing's over. The word 'over' was never uttered.

I did love Myriam, and Myriam did love me. She left me ... But didn't I do everything I could to get her to leave me?

We left each other. And we parted on good terms. Take heart. No violence, no unnecessary cruelty, not wanting to hurt one another, and no words spoken to be regretted later.

Myriam merely asked me to let her have a little time:

— I want to think about things, Paul.

– Sure.

– I'll call you when . . .

– You will?

– I'll call you. Give me a bit of time.

Is a love affair over when one of the two asks for time to think about things?

Myriam hasn't called me. Not yet. But there's no reason why she won't call me one of these days.

What'll I do then? Will I tell her I still love her?

Yes, definitely. Because I do still love her.

And what'll she say?

Will she say what she said the first time I dared to say to her 'I love you'?

Nothing. But she mimed a great whoosh of violins and raised an invisible trumpet to her lips, intoning a sort of *Marseillaise*: 'Pa-la-pa-lam-pa-la-pa-la-pam-pam-pa-la-pa-la-pam-pa-la-lam . . .!' And half-waltzed on the pavement, spinning around me . . .

And then she kissed me.

On the next page of my notebook, this:

For as far back as I can remember, I've always loved words.

I'd thought of starting with these words, but not for long. I crossed them out, mercilessly: pompous and pretentious, which is what Mr Hamel would doubtless have put in the margin. You instantly come across as boastful as soon as you start on this topic. Expressing your love of words, and listing the books you've read seems almost more boastful than bragging about your sexual exploits, real or imagined. 'Fuck it, Paulou, you stuck-up little shit! You don't really expect me to believe you've read all those books, yo, motherfucker. I don't believe you, man, you're just bragging!'

As I've taken the plunge and confessed, I have to mention, if only briefly, that shameful disease I contracted as a boy: a passion for reading,

Who gave me the virus? My father, definitely. He read a lot. History books, mainly, discoveries, colonization, the Arab civilization, the lives of famous people, the kings of France, Napoleon, de Gaulle . . . Books were sacred for him. He handled them with such religious respect! He was always borrowing books from the French Railway's library. The covers were already protected, but the first thing he did when he got home was to cover them with cellophane. He was terrified one of his sons would make them dirty or lose them, and then he wouldn't be able to return them by the due date. Whenever he discovered that the borrowed volume had been soiled or manhandled by a previous reader, he would be furious. He was tormented by the thought that he might be accused of having done such a thing. Worse still, that one of his colleagues could have done such a barbaric thing – 'Someone who works for the railways!' So he'd try to mend the damage, smoothing creased pages and gluing unstitched spines and bindings back together, and erasing notes in the margin and greasy finger marks. As if to instill the idea in us that there's something human about books, he would say: 'This poor book's been tortured.' Tortured.

We had to wash our hands before we touched any book, and reading in the kitchen was forbidden, to make sure it didn't get stained. I don't think my father ever turned down the corner of a page in all his life, or left a book lying open, face down, or underlined a word, even with a pencil. He even covered the paperbacks he bought. He wasn't a religious man, didn't observe any of the rites apart from not eating pork, but he bought his bookmarks from the little shop at the mosque – those leather bookmarks with the Prophet's name engraved in gold on them. Even the most insignificant paperback was as holy as the Koran for him.

And the worst spanking my brother ever got, when he was four or five, was for having torn an atlas. I was already drawing my treasure islands, I was coloring the earth pink and yellow, and the sea blue. I would draw a cross to mark the spot where the pirates had buried the chest . . . Daniel wanted to go one better, I guess, by taking hold of whole countries and continents!

* * *

For as far back as I can remember . . . I could read. At the age of three, if Ma is to be believed, sitting on my father's knees, I pretended I could decipher what was on the page – those little things wriggling black on white fascinated me. Then I asked him to teach me. And before long I wanted 'books for grown-ups'. I might or might not have understood what I read, but I rarely gave up on a book because I found it boring, or because it was too difficult for me. I was happier being bored and finishing it. I made it a point of honor. A funny quirk that made the guys on the block think I was stuck up.

– Paulou, you coming? We're going skating.

– No, wait! I haven't finished my book.

– *M'dereh*! Shee-it! I haven't finished my book!

Buying books was a big to-do.

Like her sister Zaïa, Ma never went into bookstores, and my father found it a bit awkward too. He didn't feel at ease there. He felt less intimidated when he borrowed books from the library. I was a bit like him. And maybe I subconsciously wanted to get my revenge for years of frustration when I cussed out the Abbess. She was a bookseller running a bookstore, and she epitomized all booksellers. Maybe I wanted to wash away an insult. She, or someone like her, was the bookseller my father had asked for a copy of Herman Melville's *Dominique* for me, who'd answered, with a snigger:

– You mean *Moby Dick*, I suppose! It was Fromentin who wrote *Dominique*. Anyway, if it's for this little nipper, he's not old enough. Why not give him *The Little Prince*?

(This little nipper!)

A few days before Christmas, or before my birthday,
I'd make a list of books I wanted and give it to Ma, who'd
give it to my aunt, who'd give it to her brother-in-law,
Mohamed. Mohamed had absolutely no qualms about
going into bookstores. Or anywhere, for that matter. He's
the loudmouth in the family. His whole attitude to life
can be summed up by a motto proclaimed to everyone in
earshot: 'They better not fuck with me!'

But it was as if he'd got me some forbidden fruit, by
way of Zaïa – my drug. And this ritual added even more
magic to the books he gave me, which made it all the
more pleasurable.

My teachers also wondered at times if I wasn't making
things up when I said I'd read this and that.

Mrs Paulet, a.k.a. Paulette:

— So, Smaïl, come to the blackboard and narrate the
story for us!

But I hated doing that. It was guaranteed to make me
clam up.

— Yo! Mistake, go on, NARRATE us a story!

Couldn't she at least have simply asked me to *tell* the
story, that heartless Paulette! But that WORD NARRATE!
To make me look even more ridiculous, on purpose.

So I would tell them a story. There again, my honor
was at stake.

I really liked Mr Hamel, my French teacher in my fourth
year, because he told us, quite to the contrary, that reading
was a personal, private affair, and a novel was not for
talking about – novels were for being read!

— The story's nothing. It's the way it's told that matters.
And the only person who can tell it properly is the author.

He didn't haul me up to the blackboard to *NARRATE*

stories. But knowing my enthusiasm for reading, he wrote to my parents and said I was welcome to come and read at his house on Wednesday afternoons, if I wanted.

If I wanted! What a question! And my astonishment, on my first visit ... I told everyone all about it in the school yard next day in the break:

— Hamel doesn't have TV!

— Wow, Paulou, no shit!

— I was in his house. He doesn't have TV! He's just got books.

— Wow, fucking pansy!

Mr Hamel was a widower, just a year or two away from his retirement. His daughter lived in America, his son in Africa. He called me – though there's no reason why I should write this in the past tense as I still visit him from time to time, and he still calls me – 'my boy'.

— How are you, my boy? What have you been up to, my boy?

He greets me with these words and shushes his dog Nestor, who barks himself silly even before I ring the bell, as soon as he hears the elevator door shut. Mr Hamel lives on Boulevard Ornano, a great heap of a red-brick building built in the '40s, on one of those estates that'll make archeologists in the centuries to come think that Stalin's dictatorship spread as far as France – the observation is his, not mine. The little I've learned about contemporary history doesn't come from my history teachers but from Mr Hamel. The lies of official history, all the falsification, the silence about the crimes committed by the Paris police during the Algerian war ... What happened on that terrible night of October 17, 1961, the night of the Arab pogrom in Paris, the night when my uncle Mehdi was killed along with more than a hundred other A-rabs, all victims of Arab-bashing. The little you can find out about it, at least. If you *want* to find out about it, that is.

— They found his body in the Seine, at Conflans, on the twenty-first, I think, or the twenty-second. My aunt Zaïa thought she was going mad. She'd had no news of him for four or five days! She didn't know if he'd been arrested or murdered . . . He wasn't demonstrating when they killed him, she's sure about that. He was on his way to work. He was a stagehand at the Olympia. He had a license to drive after the curfew. Besides, he wasn't Algerian.

— That day, my boy, all it took was having skin that was a little bit dark, and hair a bit frizzy . . .

— Like me.

— Like you, my boy.

I appreciated the way Mr Hamel called me 'my boy' but talked to me 'like a man'. He didn't try to paint a rosy picture of life . . . But he offered me disgusting vanilla wafers that I hated but didn't dare refuse, and grenadine, which he mixed any old how, sometimes pouring in far too much syrup, sometimes not enough. And when I brought him sweets made by Zaïa, he put the package on a shelf in the hall, where he'd forget about it, sometimes until the following Wednesday.

The apartment is gloomy and untidy. Dirty windows, shutters askew, burned-out lightbulbs that never get replaced, ashtrays overflowing, empty bottles here, there and everywhere, dog hairs, tobacco, dust, sadness . . . But how happy I was every time I entered that den of books! That uplifting feeling of disembarking in uncharted lands of knowledge.

While Mr Hamel talked to me, he poured himself glass after glass of red wine. It took me a long while to realize that he was alcoholic. An alcoholic for me – a wino – is a tramp flat out on a bench, bawling out awful things. But Mr Hamel would go on quietly talking, drawing on his maize-paper Gitanes, endlessly but in vain dusting off the ash and shreds of tobacco that studded his old gray hand-knitted sweater. And the more he drank, the more profound he seemed to get. He was the only one who managed to find the right words to say to me when my father died. Or when I talked to him about Daniel, and how worried I was about him. Or Myriam. Sometimes he interrupted me:

– Wait, my boy!

And then he took a book, turned the pages, and quickly found what he was looking for . . . It's all in literature. It's all been said. In some book or other you'll always find an allusion to what's happening, the proof that others have suffered what you're suffering, that you're not alone in the world. In some book or other you'll always find something like consolation.

How old was I? . . . Fifteen? Sixteen? One day, I got to his house very late, and in a really bad mood because once again some cops had asked me for my papers and taken me off to the station without telling my parents, and searched me, and called me boy and asshole and wog, and threatened to ram a stick up my ass if I hit back – for nothing, for no reason other than the pleasure of arresting a darkie! They claimed I looked like a young dealer who had just moved into the the neighborhood. To the police, all *beurs*, every single one of them, look like all the dealers they're after, whatever race they belong to – white, yellow, or black – just as long as they've been reported! Whatever their height, shape, age, and regardless of any distinguishing features marked on the record! Mr Hamel took the volume with *The Merchant of Venice* from his complete works of Shakespeare and read me Shylock's tirade, translating it as he went along:

– 'If you prick us, do we not bleed? . . . If you poison us, do we not die? And if you wrong us, shall we not revenge? If we are like you in the rest, we will resemble you in that . . .'

I came home from Mr Hamel's very proud, my heart fired with enthusiasm, steeped with the feeling that I was much cleverer than I'd been three hours earlier. Any cops would have been ill advised to arrest me then! I'd have recited Shakespeare at them! 'If you wrong us, shall we not revenge?'

And later, in bed, before putting the light out, I called out to my topman perched on the foreyard up there:

– You asleep, Queequeg?

– No, not yet.

– You know what Mr Hamel told me?

Then I tried to repeat the things Mr Hamel had told me, but I soon muddled everything up. Daniel obligingly murmured vague 'Mmm . . . Mmm . . . Mmm' sounds.

Then I realized he was asleep. Sleep came to me, too. The anchor was weighed for the land of dreams. Mr Hamel was pouring grenadine onto the carpet, we were floundering about up to our ankles in syrup, everything was soft, sticky, and ashy all at once, someone was ringing the doorbell, Nestor barked. Cops on the landing, saying they'd come looking for young Smaïl, Paul, for an ID check.

Myriam – again.

No, the next installment soon. I can hear drunken yelling, insults, and threats being hurled in God knows what Scandinavian language spiked with Hs and Ks . . . Noise of people charging down the stairs like a single mass of flesh, and screams, the couple I'd given number twelve to, a big fat fair-haired slob about six feet six tall, and made even taller by his stilettos, and his partner – a drag queen, I'm sure – who he brought with him from his northern mists. She – if that's the right word – answers him back in his own tongue. They hit each other, rolling around on the floor, and she gets the upper hand. I rush to intervene, with the first weapon that comes to hand: the whistle. To subdue them I say:

– Stop it or I call *Polizei*!

Why German? *Polizei*? God knows. I must have thought it would calm them down that much quicker. And maybe police in Swedish or Norwegian is *Polizei* . . . I say again:

– *Polizei*!

But nothing happens, so I press the button on the whistle, which was meant to emit unbearable ultrasonic sounds . . . Nothing. I push harder: nada. Péquod must have given me a dud.

I fell on the two men and tried to separate them. She lashed out with a violent blow from her elbow in the . . . *Ow*! Piercing pain! That'll teach me to remember to wear a box outside the ring: the real bouncers, the front-line rosebuds, the SS heavies like Farid and Samir-the-Heavyweight, always remember to protect themselves down there (SS = Security Service).

The male half of the couple had a bleeding mouth, the woman was raining blows on him, using as a weapon one of her red high-heeled shoes. I crawled toward the desk – the cosh, the spray. I got to my feet, pounced on them, and sprayed them with orthochlorobenzal. Their eyes started to water, and they were coughing and choking, and finally they stopped hitting each other – to catch their breath.

My eyes were also watering. And it was just then that Péquod loomed into view, enraged, a sleeve of his jacket ripped – his superb white crinkled mock-croc jacket, with its big gold zips. And his eyes started to water, too! And he was coughing! The fumes from the *inhibitor spray* . . . (that's what's written on the can).

At the time I didn't understand one word of what he was shouting at me – something about me going with him and sorting out some drag queen who'd attacked him . . . (Him, too?)

– What the fuck are they doing here, those two? he said, pointing at the stunned Scandinavians.

He didn't wait for my answer. Still reeling from the shock of what he'd just been through, he repeated:

– I was parking my Cherokee on the sidewalk where trannies cruise, and this old fuck of a drag queen pulls open my door and – pow! – slashes my . . . D'you see it? The bitch! Bitch! Claims my wing mirror touched him! His rubber tits, yeah! Fuck it . . . You come with me! I'll give that sucker something to remember . . .

I protested on two counts. One: I couldn't leave my desk, not after what had just happened. And two: Just the two of us, against the gang of trannies cruising a bit farther along, didn't stand much of a chance, except if we went in with guns – but that wasn't included in my conditions of employment:

– You took me on as a night watchman at *Le Modern'*, I said, not as a bodyguard.

– You . . . you . . . you . . .

Péquod was stammering, his voice choking. He put his hand on his heart. Suddenly I was afraid he was going to have a heart attack . . . Then something else came up and saved him, and me: the Scandinavian queen had pushed his injured man into the elevator all lovey-dovey now and whispering sweet nothings, when, by mistake, or to piss us off a bit more, he set the alarm off.

The fire brigade would be round in three or four minutes. Péquod rushed to turn the buzzer off and snapped at me:

– Dial 18 and tell them not to come!

18 was busy.

An English customer in a pink chiffon baby doll nightie riding up above his crack, red as a rare steak, high on fear, tore down the stairs . . .

– Fire!

. . . followed by a black hooker in a leopard-skin stretch jump suit.

Me:

– No, it's nothing! False alarm! Er . . . Wrong alarm! Quiet!

The hooker:

– Quiet, they're telling you! There's no fire!

The phone rang.

Péquod:

— Get it, Paul!

— Hello.

— Montmartre fire station . . .

— Ah, thanks, no, it's a false alarm! Don't come! A mistake, some drunk who . . . Thanks for calling. Thanks a lot.

Péquod tried to persuade the English guy to go back up to his room, casting mean glances at the African whore . . . then at his night watchman. The English guy refused: No way was he going back to his room. He wanted us to bring his things down, he'd get dressed down here in reception. He refused to wind up the night 'in such a dump.'

The whore then cursed him with all the nasty names from his country . . . But Péquod told me to chuck her out. I had to grab the poor thing bodily, like a cop (*Heichma*, Paul!). She screamed that she wanted to get her raincoat first. She struggled with me, scratching my hands and cheeks. I promised her I'd go get her coat if she'd calm down . . . I ran upstairs to her room, number fifteen, and raced back down with her coat, and handed it to her:

— There you are!

— Fuck off now! Péquod hissed at her, full of loathing.

Then I had to go back upstairs to number fifteen, stuff all the English guy's things into his travel bag, bring them back down for him, and suffer the humiliation of him checking and rechecking to make sure I hadn't forgotten – or stolen – anything . . .

— No, sir, I'm not a thief.

He put his clothes back on behind the reception desk and left in a dignified way, without so much as a word, his shoulder bag bouncing on his beer-belly – and that was another lucky thing, that rooms were always paid for in advance at Le *Modern'*, I could almost hear Péquod thinking. I found the idea amusing that that diaphanous pink baby doll nightie freak reckoned it was less danger-ous to roam the streets of Pigalle at three in the morning than to go back to his all-mod-cons room in *Le Modern'*.

Péquod was finally in a position to vent his wrath. I knew damn well I'd be the scapegoat, and that I'd have to pay for his jacket ripped by a tranny.

– Why d'you let that black whore go upstairs? he shouted at me.

I tried to keep my cool, and replied calmly:

– She looked OK. I thought she was on the level . . .

– On the level! A cow in leopard-skin Lycra! A black hooker!

– She had her raincoat over her. How was I to know? She looked like a harmless hooker to me . . . Quiet. And the guy with her. Could well have been her regular guy, almost!

– You taking the piss out of me? A Senegalese tart! A black whore! Fat ass . . .! I don't want their sort here. Those Senegalese girls are just AIDS holes! What's more, they're shacked up with a bunch of thugs . . .

– How was I to know? She wasn't talking Wolof to him! And I'd never seen her round here, that one, I'd never seen her before. I don't know her! *Had zahafni*! On my word!

– Hey, don't get smart with me, or I'll flip.

– And then the guy, he knows what he's up to . . .

— You're not answering me!

— He knows what he's doing, right, when he picks up a hooker. It's not my business! Once he's paid for his bed!

— She scratched you? Let me see! You'll be lucky if you didn't pick up HIV!

He didn't say aitch-eye-vee but ran the three letters forming the fearsome acronym together, so they came out sounding like the name 'Yves.' That made me laugh when I realized what he meant. Péquod looked a bit taken aback. I made the most of my temporary advantage and let fly a direct hit in his stomach – a verbal direct hit, I mean:

— Listen, I said to him, kind of solemn, with the tone of voice of one whose dignity has been offended, if you want me to resign, I will. If you don't trust me anymore . . .

That did the trick! He protested, surprised, and suddenly all conciliatory:

— No, no. That'll do for now. Let's forget about it.

— Thanks, I said coldly.

Paul Smaïl wins on points.

But to get the last word in, a low blow to his opponent, below the belt – and how! – Péquod added:

— As for sorting out the queen, I'll find a man, a real man, with balls!

And he walks off into the night, up Rue des Martyrs, white and gold! Like a reptile! Sparkling!

Earlier I wrote that, most of the time, nothing ever happened at *Le Modern*', which gave me time to write. Most of the time – yes.

Up early, next morning. A quick glance at the screens: all quiet on board, decks and gangways empty, nobody in the video room watching *Coitus! Coitus!* No sign of another mutiny. Five rooms stayed empty, the customers who came didn't look too fired up, and there weren't any black hookers – because Péquod doesn't want any, that's the way it is. An Italian turned up with a West Indian part-time whore I know, an easygoing chick, but I told him, '*hotelo completo.*' (*Balek*, watch out, Paul, goodie-goodie! Go by the book! Safety first! No more risks! Premise: All black chicks are whores and AIDS holes, just like all *beurs* are thieves and dealers.) With *Le Modern*' becalmed, I can pick up where I left off . . .

So – *Myriam* . . .

Two days after my stormy exit from Ms. Moriot's – the tight-assed Abbess, Book Bitch, Ms Ann Thrope, bleeding-heart liberal commie bitch: I was forever saddling her with derogatory and ridiculous nicknames while I settled my beef with her – at about 7.30 p.m. I went to spy on Myriam at the entrance to the Abbesses Métro station. That's how daring I was.

My heart was beating faster than after nine three-minute sessions with the skipping rope. My hands were sweaty, my mouth dry.

She saw me before I saw her:

– Paul. Are you waiting for someone?

90

– I was waiting for you. I took the liberty of . . . I wanted to apologize.

– Apologize for what? You don't need to apologize! Not to me. I'm just a bit sad that . . .

– What . . .?

– Well, that you're no longer with m . . . with us, I mean . . .

(But you definitely caught that fleeting m . . ., Paul! You definitely heard that 'me' so discreetly sidestepped in the nick of time.)

– Yes . . .?

– And that you lost your job so soon! But it's true she's a pain in the ass!

(She, who's so well brought up, said 'ass', Paul).

I agree:

– A right pain in the ass.

– The way she . . . When she introduced you as . . .

– As the pizza boy?

– No, you know what I mean . . .

– Yes, I know, Myriam.

– When I first met her, she asked me how my parents had survived during the war. One of the very first things she asked me! But if you could have held on a bit longer, you . . .

– I'm not keeping you, am I?

– No, but it doesn't matter anyway. I mean . . .

('No, but it doesn't matter anyway!' You heard it right, Paul.)

– I . . . Can I buy you a drink?

– Yes, that'd be nice.

And it all seemed so easy and unreal! Serious and frivolous, moving and happy, everything shimmering with slips of the tongue and dappled with things not said. In the grip of the magic of the moment, I forgot about feeling ill at ease and dwelling on my usual anxieties: do I smell? am I too crude? don't I come across too much like a Moroccan Barbès A-rab? As if my outburst in the bookstore, two days earlier, had taken a whole load off my chest.

But I just couldn't shake off one particular obsession: Would I be able to resist my desire to kiss Myriam? And should I resist my desire to kiss her? How far could I go? And I had a split second of absurd panic when the waiter came and took our order:

— Tea with lemon, Myriam said to him.

And me, who hates tea:

— Er . . . same as you . . . Two teas with lemon, please.

Man, did I want a beer!

After a quarter of an hour, seeing that I was still not pouring what was in my teapot into my cup, Myriam observed:

— You like it cold and really strong?

Me:

— What?

— Your tea.

— No, I don't like tea, period.

— So why did you . . .?

— Because I'm an idiot!

Our laughter, then, the tender way she looked at me, that pretty way she had of hiding behind her hands – the memory's still intact, clear, and forever.

There was a lull in the conversation. Several lulls . . . But that airy silence wasn't unpleasant. I felt I had wings, and I was happy. God knows why I started talking again! Especially when it was to ask her:

— So what d'you think of me?

(*Rhmale!*)

She protested, quite rightly:

— Good heavens, what a thing to ask! I hardly know you . . . I don't know you, really. How can I know what to think of you? Anyway, I'm not here to pass judgment on you.

— I mean . . . how d'you see me?

— Well . . . someone who's a bit ill at ease, someone who's so ill at ease, in fact, that he can ask a question like that! There's so much anger in you . . . Don't take it the wrong way if I tell you you're a bit scary! It seems you enjoy scaring people, but it's obvious too that . . .

— What . . .?

— Nothing.

— I scare you?

— A bit, yes. How should I put it? Your anxiety makes me feel a bit anxious, too. But I . . . .

— Yes, tell me!

— No, nothing. People need a bit more time, Paul.

They say that everything, in love, is said on the very first day. Afterward, people just repeat the very first theme, over and over again, in all possible permutations.

'Give me a bit more time.' That's the last thing Myriam said to me, the very last time.

But when we left the café, that first time, she said:

— I've got to run!

I thought I heard a note of distress in those words. She had to run away, in the fullest sense of the words. And I, also, sensed a great sadness.

Very well then, so be it! I'm head over heels in love. Desperately and happily in love. Happy and unhappy all at once. Scared shitless that things will fall apart at the first hiccup and yet quite sure that things will last a lifetime. I'm absurdly in love, but aren't people always absurdly in love when they're in love? Aren't people always a bit ridiculous? Or romantic, which is the same thing. 'Pa-la-pa-lam-pa-la-pa-la-pam-pam . . .!'

Bursts of happiness and split seconds of sadness, I go along with it all. I learn how to give, and – which is harder – to receive. I still have to learn not to be ashamed of myself anymore, to be less angry and uptight, less on my guard – Myriam tells me as much, and I have to listen to her. You have to love yourself a little bit in order to love somebody else. I have to stop scrutinizing myself the way I do, stop blowing into my palms to make sure I don't have bad breath, stop wondering if I'm dressed well enough, stop combing my hair again and again . . . But I also have to stop losing my temper so violently, and shaking my fist at those assholes honking their horns because we don't cross the road quickly enough, arm in arm . . . When I'm with her, stop calling all assholes assholes!

My pad is a thousand square feet – with shower, stove, sink, and *mirhad* – a sixth-floor walk-up, no elevator, view over the backyard, on Boulevard Barbès, above Berbersol – *You'll always find bargains at Berber*! –

and I have to pluck up the courage to invite Myriam over without feeling humiliated. After all, I've invited girls up before Myriam, more middle-class girls than Myriam, and I didn't give a damn, then, about what they might think of the decor. As long as they were more or less willing . . . In other words, ready to get laid, whether it was spelled out *before* or not.

Where could we go other than my place? Myriam lived with her folks, near Place de la République, on top of which, she was an only child. My only concession would be to say my room instead of my pad, and your parents instead of your folks.

But, needless to say, the first time I finally plucked up the courage to ask Myriam up to my room, I screwed up – a total fiasco, as Stendhal would have put it.

To put it like Smaïl would put it: I flopped, I couldn't get it up. Impossible to keep up the act. Half a hard-on. A pretend erection . . . *Oualou*. Too limp to slip on a condom. Flustered hours spent talking a lot of gibberish. Until Myriam whispered in my ear:

– Paul, it doesn't matter.

But, without meaning to boast about it, getting a hard-on had never been a problem for me up to then. I lost my virginity with a girl from my third-year class, at her place, which means in her mother's place – her mother wasn't there – one Wednesday afternoon. Léopoldine – her name was Léopoldine – told me afterward that I'd been (and I quote) 'great, much cooler than William.' And ever since then, getting it on had never been a problem. Always blonds. I'd get all worked up, then I'd come – that was it. Simple matter of health, physical and mental. At Nanterre, I never found a better way of beating boredom. I had some great flings that lasted a few hours, and even a whole night now and then! And come the morning, *ciao*! My longest scene lasted three weeks – Claire. And *pace* Stendhal again if I wax a bit vulgar: She was the best fuck I ever had. Which probably explains why it lasted so long.

I'm not proud of it, believe me. I would say as much to Daniel, when he was worried because he still hadn't slept with a woman, in the days when he hadn't quite figured out why he still hadn't slept with a woman:

– Any stupid fuck can jack off, you know! What's harder is not to lay a chick but to lay *with* a chick . . . But the hardest thing of all is definitely loving a woman.

The oddest thing was that I would always talk theoretically in those days, without having experienced love – real, true love. Without knowing that very strong feelings can cause temporary impotence. Was this the famous *crystallization* thing? I was petrified. Mortified. This involuntary chastity drove me crazy. No matter how often Myriam told me it didn't matter, I didn't believe her – I had to get it up. Knowing all the time, too, that the more I thought about it, the less chance I'd have of getting it up. We talked about it, and I ended up laughing – but it was phony laughter.

– What's more, there we were sounding just like people on those TV talkshows and in those lousy tabloids: breakdown in bed – what's the remedy. And I would chant, trying to appear composed: 'Breakdown in bed/ Don't lose your head . . .'

– Paul, you're crazy.

How could we possibly have thought that the answer was to introduce me to Mr and Mrs Fink, her parents?

Myriam had already raised the subject two or three times, but not in a pushy way. She said they'd like to meet me. I resisted the idea. I didn't say yes or no. I would always find one reason or another to get out of it. I dreaded the thought of the examination awaiting me. Because I couldn't imagine the meeting other than as an examination, an inspection, an observation, an appraisal, an estimation – *'an-nadjda*!

Realizing that one more evasive answer would hurt Myriam, I finally capitulated. I couldn't get out of it any longer!

– OK, for a drink, one evening, before supper. But just a drink.

To think of the anxiety that overcame me as soon as I woke up on the appointed judgment day! I had a consuming desire to call Myriam at the bookstore and make up any old excuse to get out of it! I even started hoping for a serious accident – like my father suddenly dying, or God knows what! And that nervous tic I thought I'd got rid of – blowing my breath up into my nose – came back with a vengeance. The impression of smelling of sweat, fat, burned food, the melted cheese on the pizzas, the synthetic fabric of my delivery boy's uniform. Barbès! A phobia, a truly obsessive nightmare. I brushed my teeth, again and again, I washed my hands over and over, I polished and repolished my black shoes, I combed and recombed my hair, I shaved three times. Should I wear a tie, my one and only silk tie? Should I take flowers? Would it be bad form to ask Myriam if I ought to take flowers?

My mind's made up – I'm bound to screw up, royally. These people are Jewish, they won't be able to stand the sight of me. And I won't know what to say. And if they ask me things, I know I'm bound to miss the point and say things I shouldn't say in front of them. It goes without saying that they'll be polite to me, but they'll still see me as the nasty piece of work who's stealing their darling daughter from them! Their only daughter! Their only child! By force! Even if Myriam's over eighteen! Even if she's already been out with other men!

Even if she's already been out with other men, I'm her first Arab! An Arab's stealing their daughter! Meaning: raping their . . . (An impotent rapist, but they don't know that.) An Arab! Maybe pro-Palestinian! A supporter of the Intifada! A bomber! A killer! . . . Who's just used up a whole tube of toothpaste.

— Shall we go?

— Let's go.

Myriam and I had arranged to meet by an exit at the République Métro station. We walked side by side, not saying a word. I didn't have any flowers and I wasn't wearing a tie. She seemed to approve.

— This is it?

— This is it.

We went in and climbed the stairs to the first floor. She gave the doorbell three quick rings before turning her key in the lock.

— Daddy, Mummy, here's Paul!

— Come in, sir, please.

The worst thing was that Mr and Mrs Fink looked even more embarrassed than I felt. I tried reversing the situation and imagining my own parents greeting Myriam. They'd be incredibly intimidated, too! Thinking about them should have helped me get through the ordeal, but no such luck. The Finks were so kind and smiling, they did everything possible to make me feel at ease, but so much so that all it did was increase my embarrassment and theirs.

— Take a seat, sir, please!

— Mummy, you can call him Paul.

— Would you like . . . There's whiskey, gin, Martini. Maybe you'd rather have a glass of white wine? I think there's some in the refrigerator.

— Er . . . I . . . Er . . . Just . . . A . . . Yes, a . . . Mart . . . A whiskey . . . Just a drop . . . Thank you . . . Thank you very much.

— Ice?

— Er . . . N'yes . . . No, I, yes . . . er . . . If you . . . Yes. Thank you. Thank you very much.

Mr Fink poured me a good third of the bottle of J&B into a large cut-glass tumbler. His hands were flecked with gold. He was a bookbinder at the government publications office. Mrs Fink was the spitting image of her daughter and hardly seemed any older. Myriam had told me they were often taken for sisters, and now I understood why.

— Myriam's told us all about you, she said shyly to me, holding out a bowl of olives. (No, no olives, Paul! You won't know what to do with the stone.) 'All about you.'

But she didn't know what to say next . . . Neither did I.

Nor Mr Fink. It was Myriam who saved the day by talking about her lover's brilliant studies, making her lover blush. He gulped down a great slug of whiskey, choked, stood up to get his breath back, and nearly knocked over a lamp standing on a pedestal table – *balek! balek!* The living room wasn't very big, and it was cluttered with pretty little pieces of furniture and fragile knickknacks. Luff up! Heave to port! Ready about!

– What beautiful books you have, I said, even more astonished than the others at being able to string seven syllables together in one fell swoop. (Well done, Paul, top marks for originality!)

– If you're interested in books, Mr Fink replied, you ought to come and see me at the government publications office.

And Mrs Fink, with the half-daring, half-panic-stricken gestures of a young girl jumping off the high diving board for the first time in her life:

– Will you stay for supper?

KO! Smaïl the light heavyweight! Punch-drunk but still standing!

Stupefied, I brought Myriam into focus through a kind of dizzy blur, going no no no no no with my eyes, with her going yes yes yes yes yes . . . And I ended up hearing myself answer, quite against my better judgment:

– That's very kind of you. Thank you. I'd like to very much. (Fink: one point.)

No way I can remember anything about that supper: what I ate, what I drank, our conversation – if there was one. Just a vague recollection of how I congratulated myself after successfully negotiating every obstacle. I didn't spill food on myself, I didn't use the wrong cutlery, I didn't knock the salt-cellar over, and, as I'd seen people do in films, I got politely to my feet when I saw Mrs Fink get up from the table to go to fetch a dish or to clear away the plates.

— Paul, please! You're too well brought up. We're just family here.

(Visitor: one point.)

But after supper we got involved in a conversation I remember better. I was touched by their kindness, and my gratitude was somewhat effusive. These people didn't feel obliged to talk, like so many people do, about our origins, our cultural differences, the problems facing young people trying to get a foothold in our society – right? And all it would take would be a little goodwill – right? And blah-blah-blah.

No, they were tactful. They didn't smother me with the phony niceness of those who want you to know loud and clear that they're not racists, that they don't have prejudices – the Abbesses! If they were curious about me, they were curious in a discreet way. They didn't judge me. They didn't ask me what my plans were for later on in life, or what my parents did. I wasn't taking some exam. The Finks were good people.

— You see, it wasn't such a terrible ordeal, Myriam whispered as she walked me to the front door.

I whispered back:

— It's not very late. Won't you walk with me a little way . . .

She took an umbrella and told her parents not to wait up for her.

We walked across the Place de la République. We were humming in the rain. At each traffic light we kissed as we waited to cross the road, and sometimes, when the light was red, we waited until it went green, then red again, then green, so we could keep on kissing. The Christmas lights shone just for us. The rain fell just for us. The stupid jerk in his yellow GTI honked just for us . . . But I didn't call him a stupid asshole or threaten him with a rod up his ass, son of a bitch!

Boulevard de Magenta, in front of the Face-à-Face window, pointing at Tradition, the most old-fashioned wedding gown in a whole window full of frothy wedding gowns, Myriam shrieked, laughing:

— I want that one!

And in front of the disused Luxor I said:

— When I was little, I thought it was a real Egyptian palace, from the time of the pharaohs, and I thought those mummies were buried under the cinema seats! I can't remember who told me that nonsense.

As we walked under the subway bridge, a train passed, and we took advantage of the hellish din to scream like lunatics. And it felt good.

We walked back up Boulevard Barbès and came to Berbersol.

— Coming?

— Yes.

We raced up the stairs two at a time, up to the sixth floor, where we collapsed out of breath onto my bed. And then we started to caress each other and undress each other, caressing all the while and gazing into each other's eyes. And we made love. And it was good. It was very good. Perfect harmony. Then we started all over again, and it was just as good the second time around. It was my turn to sing the *Marseillaise*:

— Pa-la-pa-lam-pa-la-pa-la-pam-pam-pa-la-pa-la-pam-pa-la-lam . . .!

What more can I say? How can I describe the months that followed, the laughter and the tears, the stolen kisses, hand in hand, lipstick on my cheek, the silences, the clouds, the storms, the bright spells, the fleeting quarrels and the passionate reunions? The fleeting reunions and the passionate quarrels . . . Little by little I got the feeling something was about to snap . . . Something *had* snapped. A sinking feeling. Of being lost. Neither with you nor without you. There's no choice, no freedom anymore. The horror of spending all day wondering if I should call or not. Crying in a café listening to Oum Kalsoum singing about the pain of being in love . . . But also about how love opens the gates to paradise: *Djena* – the only word in the chant that I understand.

The time had come to part. We'd met in October, and we parted in June. What else is there to say? Haven't I suffered enough recalling that lost happiness? All the tenderness of love, Myriam's presence, her gentleness and affection, they're all still floating about here in this room where, using the computer I borrowed from Péquod, I put some order in everything I jotted down last night at *Le Modern'*. I click on SAVE. I click on CLOSE. Enough.

Melville, Conrad, Stevenson, my writers, they all had the right idea: only men on board! No women. No trivial tales of love between a man and a woman to narrate! The whale hunt, the treasure hunt, the heart of darkness . . . piece of cake!

At Nanterre, I looked desperately for a course on this subject: the love narrative, the description of love, the representation of love in Western literature, love novels . . . Nothing on the bulletin board. Nowhere at Nanterre where anyone talks about love, no place where you might learn how to talk about it, or learn how to write about love. No module on the topic, not a hint of a credit course.

Nothing about sex, either. I'm the only person who stubbornly insists on pronouncing *Paris-X* as if it's a capital X and not the Roman numeral. And, incidentally, it's never made anyone laugh, either, apart from me.

Sometimes I would ask a student who looked a tiny bit less moronic than the average – I'm not putting the standard very high – if they didn't find it weird that there were no courses about the theme of love in literature. Their answer was unanimous: Love in books is a fucking bore.

Anyway, I never, I swear, never met anyone at Nanterre who liked to read.

And I tell myself that, basically, it's a stroke of luck there's no course on the subject. Literary studies seemed designed to put you right off literature. But it would have been the last straw if Nanterre put me right off loving, too.

Misfortune started to descend upon the family just after that. It was as if I had to be punished, one day, for having yearned, for one split second, for a disaster to get out of Myriam's parents' invitation.

I'm not superstitious. I don't believe in God, but I came to think that I'd brought on the wrath of the Almighty. I was invaded by a growing sense of guilt.

Daniel's gloom and melancholy seemed to grow in proportion to his muscles. He would crack up over the slightest thing, coming apart just like the stitching on his shirts. Ma was forever sewing buttons back on for him, and cooking him turkey and chicken fillets. He'd progressed from L to XL to XXL, and now bought his underpants and string vests from a specialist bodybuilders' shop. He would plant himself in front of the mirror in our parents' bedroom, or the mirror in the hall, posing, and then burst out sobbing, without anybody understanding quite why.

Meanwhile my father was going downhill. He was losing weight, he ate less and less, and often he would throw up the little he'd managed to swallow at Ma's urging.

Now the potions of our good fairy Zaïa were no use to him any longer. Zaïa, what's more, no longer wanted to give him her witch's brews. She urged him to see a doctor and have himself properly examined in the hospital. My father told her not to get too alarmed: It would all pass, he was just a bit tired, women could never understand that, they dramatized everything for no reason.

If he played down his health problems and refused to seek treatment, it wasn't so much out of fatalism as to avoid worrying us. He never took care of his own needs. And he kept his worries to himself: making ends meet, his sons on the dole, the railway company's ever harsher demands for output, Daniel's fragile state, Ma letting her sadness get the upper hand . . . And his own health.

I think he suspected his condition was serious, but the father and head of the family must never fall ill, mustn't show the slightest sign of weakness.

Ma wanted to protect Daniel, first and foremost: We mustn't upset the baby. The baby was twenty-one years old, five feet eleven inches tall, and weighed a hundred and seventy-five pounds . . . then a hundred and ninety . . . then two hundred . . . She always saw him as a scrawny kid who toiled away at school and plunged so easily into despondency.

With me you could tell the truth: I was the oldest, I would be head of the family when my father passed on. Ma respected me more but loved me less than she did my brother.

When she announced to me 'Dad's going to stay two or three days under observation. I've told Daniel it's nothing to worry about . . .' I didn't want to know any more. As if nothing unusual was going on. As if, all of a sudden, I hadn't heard anything. And in a way I hadn't heard anything.

I was bored to death at Nanterre. Winter mornings, taking the train was like embarking on the journey to the end of the night . . . And arriving in the middle of nowhere: Paris-X, yes. Thirty years before, there were shantytowns for North Africans in these parts, and hostels for immigrant workers: Was it just as sinister in those days? Maybe not. Surely not. What the hell was I doing there? Learning what? And to do what, later? I had two or three interesting courses at most. Otherwise I managed on my own: all it took was an ability to read, pencil at the ready. I asked for an exemption from regular three-monthly assessments, preferring the end-of-year exam – getting rid of that chore in one fell swoop . . . And effortlessly, if possible. (It *was* possible.)

Coming back from Paris-X was like returning. From some squalid godforsaken dump in the depths of the boonies. Rimbaud disembarking at Charleville, Rimbaud arriving in Paris!

These are cities! These are a people for whom those Alleghanys and Lebanese of dreams rose up!

Noise, rhythm, lights, real life! After a few hours at Nanterre, nothing could depress me. Even delivering pizzas seemed more intellectually rewarding than courses 102, 208, and 382! Even hitting one of Mr Luis's punch-bags, like someone possessed!

And God knows I lashed out! God knows I was

aggressive in those days! Too much, far too much, Mr Luis warned me.

— That's not boxing! You're hitting like a piece of shit! Any old how!

I would get to the gym, run down the seven steps, change in less than three minutes, and dash across the wooden floor as if the world title were at stake, as if I was going to have the fight of my life.

If I boxed, I backed up my punches, I screamed out my anger into my gumshield, unable to control myself anymore. There was blood. I would drop my guard, and learned my lesson the hard way. But I still wouldn't calm down. I'd get back up and launch another attack. I could have killed. Mr Luis banned me from sparring for a while:

— You're training, Paul. You're not in a ring!

— What? I wasn't hitting hard!

— You're answering back? Finished. No more sparring for a month!

— OK, give me a garbage bag then!

I just had to sweat out my violence.

But why so much aggression? I'd have landed a straight right on the first person who explained to me, like some fancy psychologist, that it was because I wasn't getting laid anymore.

And yet, and yet, it was the sad truth: I *wasn't* getting laid anymore. Blonds didn't tempt me any longer. Nor did brunettes. Jewish or otherwise, *laa* – no. I didn't have any desire in me. And other pleasures of life left me cold. What else was there? Books? Books. Reading alone helped me to pull through that year.

If I think back to it, the days and the seasons back then blur into one gray haze. Gray was the color of summer, fall and then winter. I had trouble putting a date on events that didn't register. Or the series of lousy little jobs I had: in a copy shop I was on my feet for hours feeding the machines with paper and reading the counters; for two weeks I ran a newsstand for a cousin who'd gone off on holiday; I unloaded trucks, I washed dishash at The Mysterious Isle (The Mysterious Isle!). The manager was a pirate. Accompanied by Diop, I had to threaten to kill him to get my pay.

Then I found something a bit better: letter-writer, public scribe. Zaïa earned me a reputation in the neighborhood: Her nephew had brains *and* a pen. To start with, I quite enjoyed writing letters and getting paid by the sheet. Except that my fee had to be very low how much can I ask of a cleaning woman who's been abandoned by her guy/and wants to get her sofa bed and her toaster back? Or the poor jerk who's lost his papers and can't remember if he was born in Marseilles or Toulon?

But it got too depressing, so I gave it up.

I became lazy.

I became lazy and I turned into a coward: I spent less and less time in Rue Ordener. My father was either coming home from hospital/or getting ready to go back in. Ma had red eyes. In the hall, she told me in a whisper that he'd just had a row with my brother. Daniel was depressed – either extremely dejected or else hyped up, depending on the day and the time. When he was hyper, he told me he'd been out the night before with Sophie. Or Sandrine.

— Hang on, baby bro. You told me her name was Aïcha.

— No, that's another one.

Suddenly I suspected that she wasn't called Sophie or

Sandrine or Aïcha. That he was making things up, and she didn't exist at all.

I make things up, too, and I lie. I always find a good reason to split quickly with my laundry for the week, all clean.

— Dad, Ma, I've got to go to work. I'm running late. *Ciao*!

I was happy to go back to my place and be with my books again.

Ah! And I started writing a great adventure novel, in the first person . . . But I soon gave that up.

All I can remember now is the opening gambit: Smile. But I didn't get much farther than the first line. With that one word I'd said it all.

I met up with Daniel again at Speedzza. He couldn't zip up his delivery boy's red oilskin anymore.

— Damn, man, your bro, Paulou!
— What about my brother?
— Fucking hell, he's a bit pumped up, woah!
— Your mother!

One evening he came in with his hair dyed platinum blond. You could see that the dye job and the cut had been done by a right professional. And I quickly picked up that it wasn't because they didn't want to crack jokes about Daniel that Taouif, Gamal, and Mickey kept their traps shut but more because they didn't want to get into a fight with his lightweight of a brother if they started blabbing. Daniel, to all appearances, was expecting me to say something . . . But he was wasting his time.

He was now earning a bit of money at Mr Muscle exhibitions, which at least paid for his bodybuilding sessions – the vicious circle.

And then he stopped coming to Speedzza. He'd found something better. Night work. But what?

— A bouncer, you know, at a club.
— What club?
— A club.

To tell the truth, I was happier not knowing too much. Like with our father.

But one night, coming back home from Nanterre, I found an envelope slipped under my door. Inside, a five-hundred-franc note and five lines scribbled on the back of a Pigalle by Night postcard:

Paul, come and see me. I'm working at the Sexyshow 2000. It's pricey, so here's some cash. It's peanuts for me. But come along if you want to: I'm on at 11. Show starts every hour. I'm Dany. Later, around 2.30, you can wait for me at the corner of Rue des Martyrs. We can meet there. D

He'd circled the note with the outline of a bottle. The skipper of the whaler had passed the thing onto his second in command. If baby bro was having a bad time, if he wanted to talk to me, all he had to do was put a little note, like that, in a bottle – a cry for help – and I'd get the message.

Sexyshow 2000 is the biggest peep show in Pigalle – *The most outrageous show in the world*!

With two obsequious creeps at the entrance, one or the other of them, or both at once, pulling you by the sleeve under torrents of pink and green neons, touting in a Tunisian-English accent:

– Supergirls and superboys, sir! Come in! First glance free!

I told them that I'd only go in if they let go of me. They opened the doors for me, bowing as they did so. I was blasted by the sound system – an old disco hit that reminded me of something: 'I love you, baby.' At the cash register I could get three, four or five hundred francs' worth of tokens, or more. Free peep: the first peep ... twenty seconds. I gave them the five hundred. I wanted at least two hundred change, but I didn't know how to ask for it.

I could choose: a girl solo, girls in a double act, a threesome of girls, girl with boy, special s/m girl with boy. I ventured deep into the blue half-light that then turned pink, then yellow, green, and red, and I asked a hostess where I could look at Dany. She pointed me to a cabin, and with a gesture told me I should slip a few tokens into her fringed panties to thank her for telling me.

The cabin reeked like a zoo. There was a high stool with a backrest, and a roll of paper towel under the one-way mirror. When I turned the lock, the scene came to life: A girl in a corset and stiletto boots was sitting astride a man on all fours, wearing a muzzle. The scene vanished almost as soon as it had appeared, and an arrow started to flash above the slot where I had to put my tokens. I fed in a good ten: the countdown went off on the timer. The revolving scene reappeared.

With a switch, the girl whipped the man – and I say 'the man' advisedly because if that man was definitely my brother, the show looked so phony to me he could have been anyone, any man. The thickness of the glass, the lighting, the slow movement of the act, the actors' pearly makeup, all made things look unreal. I couldn't see anything sensual about it, let alone sexy. For me it was a bit like watching clowns on TV, neither more exciting nor more shocking than that – except that the clown being humiliated by a dominatrix was my very own Queequeg, my kid brother.

I left the cabin in a hurry, well before I'd used up my time. I'd seen quite enough.

I went home, read for a while, and dozed off. At about two in the morning I took five one hundred-franc notes from my stash, above the meter, and went back out to meet Queequeg on the corner of Rue des Martyrs.

He was wearing a tracksuit and looked like some sporty guy who'd been working out. His features were a bit drawn, traces of silvery makeup at the corners of his mouth and on his temples . . . When he saw me he smiled a smile – of relief.

– You made it. Thanks.

It was a child's smile. And I found him handsome all of a sudden – fair-haired like an angel.

– Where shall we go? To the Nadir?

– Whazzat?

– A bar close by, open all night.

– Head for the Nadir! Weigh anchor! Cast off! Furl the foresails!

He looked proud to know a bar I didn't know about, and he went on ahead to show me the way. Just as he'd doubtless been proud to give his big brother a big bill and write in his note: *It's pricey, so here's some cash. It's peanuts for me*.

The Nadir, with raï music and whores, was dark and smoky. We took a booth at the back.

– Hang on, I said to him, here's your five hundred back . . .

– I gave you a five-hundred note.

– Yeah, I changed it, just in case . . . But . . . I didn't make it inside.

– You didn't come? So you didn't see me then?

– No.

114

— Maybe a good thing.

— Maybe, yeah.

— Does it turn you off?

— No, no. You can do whatever you like. Hey! You're twenty-one, you're an adult. It's none of my business! You get well paid, I guess. Much better than some job training whatever. What d'you want?

— Evian.

— Evian! . . . I'll have a Leffe. What did you want to talk to me about?

— I don't want Dad to find out . . . He must never know. Never, ever! He'd kill me.

— No, better if he doesn't, much better if Dad doesn't know. He wouldn't kill you, but it's best he doesn't know.

Silence.

He drank his water in little sips. Tears welled up in his eyes. He stammered:

— I'm not gay . . .

He put on that stubborn look he had when he was young and didn't want to eat. He repeated, more insistent this time:

— I'm not gay!

— Whoever said you were gay, baby bro? I know you're not gay. First off, the Sexyshow 2000 is a place for straights. There's no guy–guy acts, no solo guys either. There's a solo chick, two chicks, a chick and a guy . . .

— But . . . So you did see me? You saw my acts?

— No, no! I told you. But I know what the Sexyshow 2000 is about. I know it's not a peep show for faggots . . .

— Don't use that word faggot!

— I'll say faggot if I want to say faggot! Yo! What d'you want me to say? Faggots? Gays? Homos? Queers? And

115

even if you were gay, huh? you'd still be my brother!

— I'm not gay.

— Fuck it, I don't believe you! You're not going to make a fuss about it, are you? You're superstud, if you must know! You're Iron Man!

— Don't take the piss out of me!

— I'm not taking the piss, Daniel! It's just. . . . Tell me why you put a message in a bottle if it wasn't a cry for help . . . With a bill in the envelope, too! What's it mean? You want me to tick you off, you want me to tell you what you're up to isn't too good and all? That it's something to be ashamed of . . . Or are you afraid – but afraid of what? The cops? The Sexyshow bouncers?

— No. But it's the worry, OK, if Dad . . .

— What d'you think I'm going to do? Give the game away? Or is that what you *want* me to do, maybe? So Dad'll punish you when he finds out? Shit, you're not, making sense, baby bro!

— No. It's not that. But if Dad . . .

— You think Dad goes to peep shows, maybe? D'you think he's ever been to a porn show, even once in his life? I'm pretty damned sure he hasn't.

— Sssh!

— Sssh, what?

— Don't talk so loud, fuck it!

— I'm not talking loud . . .

— Did you see the photos of me in the entrance there?

— No, I told you, I didn't go in.

— You can't tell it's me . . . I asked them. I'm wearing a mask . . .

— A what?

— A latex mask. I'm totally disguised. You wouldn't

116

know it was me. And what's more, it excites the maso-
chists.

— Oh, yeah? Does it pay well, at least? It's not too much
like hard work? The chick doesn't beat you too hard?

— How d'you know the chick beats me?

Damn! I gave myself away. No point trying to pull the
wool over his eyes any longer. He knew I was lying. He
looked hard at me, more surprised than angry. I couldn't
find the right word, I tried to say I was sorry just with my
eyes . . . With a smile. The damage was done. He started
to cry. I laid a hand on his shoulder, but he snapped back:

— *Chelaouam*! Leave me alone!

I put it another way:

— Does she hit or is she just pretending?

— She's pretending, he answered, sniffing. It's all show.
Most of the guys they asked at the gym didn't want to do
it; they didn't want to be humiliated. I don't give a fuck.
I don't feel anything for the chick . . . And it's like it
wasn't me.

His tears flowed thick and fast.

— But . . . your dick? I said, laughing, hoping he'd pull
himself together a bit and we'd find the complicity there
used to be between us.

— It's a false one . . . he finally said, with a dash of irony
in his voice, and there was an obvious desire on his part,
too, to pick up the threads of the conversation.

— It's great – you keep a hard-on throughout the act!

But he pulled a face and said:

— What if Ma knew?

— Ma, she'd always forgive you anything, Daniel. But
you're not going to upset her, you're not going to tell her
that . . . She'd never understand . . .

— I'm a piece of shit, he hiccuped, I'm a piece of shit. Worthless.

— Drink something. You want a beer? A whiskey?

— No. No booze.

— Shit! You're not going to lay all that on me, like Taouif and Farid! Good Muslim and a boy in a peep show.

— No, no, it's for my balance. Bodybuilders mustn't drink alcohol.

— Balance, my butt! Balance! I drink and eat anything and everything, and my health's better than yours.

— You've always been number one. You're the smartest, you work hardest, you're the fittest, you're the best at everything! Dad always says so ... You do everything better than me.

I lost my temper:

— You're lying! Dad never says things like that ... You're lying! Say you're sorry!

He refused, so I repeated:

— Say you're sorry!

He gave in and said quietly, his eyes lowered:

— I'm sorry.

I still wasn't ready to drop the subject:

— Dad never ...

He flared up in turn:

— Shit, man! I said I'm sorry ...

— Dad's very ill, Daniel.

— Zaïa told me it's stomach cancer ...

— What?

— That it's stomach cancer, very advanced.

Everything around me swayed. I felt dizzy, breathless. I stared at him, mouth agape. Daniel said in a sad voice:

— That's it. For once I know something you don't ...

You haven't seen how thin he's got? Well, there you have it. They're going to operate, but ...

— Ma knows?

— Sort of. Dad keeps telling her it's nothing serious, and she'd never dare ask a doctor.

— What about Zaïa?

— Zaïa won't tell Ma the truth, that's for sure. She's her little sister. Just like I'm your baby brother ...

— What does that mean?

He shrugged his shoulders. But suddenly there we were, baby brother and big brother, sobbing like little boys on a beach who've lost sight of their parents ... There we were, sick with fear and grief, clutching onto each other.

When I'd calmed down a bit, I said to Daniel:

— I really do think you should have a drink of something.

— Really?

— Yeah. Have a whiskey. You've got your five hundred francs ... And, you know, they can treat cancer these days, it is treatable. You can be cured.

As well as could be expected, two beers and four whiskeys later we walked out of the Nadir, arm in arm – two sailors on a spree, crying, hiccuping, and playing the fool. I said to Daniel:

— Come and crash at my place! I'll sleep on the floor. I don't care.

On Boulevard Barbès the few passers-by heard us bawling in unison:

— Lower the spanker! Hoist the jib and the flying jib! Ready about! Lee-ho! Furl! Luff!

Some cops were cruising slowly along in a patrol car, the side door open. We were sitting ducks.

Skipper:

— Got your papers?

Second in command:

— Got my papers.

But a strange thing happened: They let us go on our way without asking for our ID. For once.

There were unhoped-for remissions and then moments when things suddenly got worse. My father came out of the hospital apparently cured. Then, a few days or weeks later we had to call an ambulance, which took him to the emergency ward at Lariboisière . . . Or else he went back to Fernand Widal.

If the doctors are to be believed, they tried every possible kind of treatment. But metastasis invaded his whole body. He went bald, then his hair grew back . . . He never complained.

Ma spent long hours at his bedside, and my father had to put his foot down to make her go back home and rest and deal with the everyday chores – what was the point of staying at the hospital and doing nothing? He wanted to read a bit, and watch a good film on TV . . . I think, toward the end, he couldn't bear her constant presence, her silence. Signs of impatience would suddenly slip out.

— Go on, Leïla, get going! *Kafa*!

Zaïa brought her usual good humor along with her, her infectious cheerfulness, and whiffs of amber and patchouli.

— Yacine! You're looking pretty good, you know?

She wasn't afraid to tell the ward staff what to do if need be. What? But the sheets haven't been changed! The windows are dirty! Everybody knows you can catch something in a hospital. Well it's not surprising, seeing how badly the place is kept!

From her big embroidered velvet bag, she would pull out a duster and start wiping the bedside table. Embarrassed, my father heard her berating a nurse who, at three in the afternoon, still hadn't cleared away the lunch tray. He tried to explain to her that it wasn't the nurse's job, but she would answer back that it wouldn't have taken much all the same – whether it was her job or not.

But she also smothered them with kindness, complimented them for their patience and gentleness, as if she was the one who was ill, offered almond fritters she'd made herself to a young intern she found 'as cute as they come.'

In the corridor, she whispered in my ear that she'd just been to see a marabout by the name of Foutou Baba – the best of the lot! a saint! a genius! – and he'd predicted that her *silf* would get better – and all he'd asked for was two hundred francs. But the day before – hey! – she'd really seen off that bearded weirdo from some Koranic school who had the nerve to go from room to room, during visiting hours, reminding Muslims, or those he presumed to be Muslims, about their religious duties! She made a scene with a doctor who happened to be there. What? You let scum like that into the hospital? You let them go nagging the poor suffering souls even in their beds?

– Those priests bring nothing but trouble!

My father had other visits. Plenty of his workmates came to see him for a few minutes on their way home from work, which was just a stone's throw from Fernand Widal. And not just his Arab workmates. I'd never have thought he was so popular.

I'd go along in the afternoon or evening. We talked

about anything and everything, or we stayed silent for minutes on end . . . I liked that just as much. Sometimes I was almost happy to be there. A long way from all the commotion outside.

I filled page after page of my notebook with jottings and details that I'd remembered and was afraid of forgetting again. But then I tore them all up. What was the point? When I come across a description of somebody dying in a book I've already read, or people in mourning, I usually skip those pages, or I re-read them quickly, skipping lines. Turn the page.

Turn the page. Foutou Baba was a charlatan. Dad passed away on a Saturday afternoon, at 3.10. I was there. Or rather . . . I was in the corridor.

A little later, I went to the Sexyshow, where my brother also had performances on Saturday afternoons. I asked to see Dany (Dany!).

The person on the door told me that customers weren't permitted to meet the artistes and, in any case, Dany was getting himself ready. I said once again, in a tone of voice that was firm enough to get the guy to take me seriously:

— I want to see him right now.

He opened the door of a cabin and pushed the catch on the lock:

— There, d'you see him?

Daniel was standing in the red half-light, as if headless in his mask. He was just a body. I didn't recognize the body right away – as they say at the morgue.

But I said to the guy on the door, seizing the lapels of his jacket:

– Listen to me, I'm his brother and our father's just died, right? I'll give you one minute to go and get him behind the window, and tell him to get dressed because he's coming with me, or else I'll smash the place up, OK?
– OK.

And once again I was striding along, making my way with difficulty through the Saturday afternoon crowd, on my way to find my brother. But the people I pushed and shoved protested in German, and the streets were awash with cold drizzle that was so thick the cars had their headlights on full beam, and night was falling, and I was walking along a canal that was a flooded roadway, possibly, because you couldn't see where the road ended and the water began, and I walked under the elevated metro bridge to a station that wasn't called Barbès-Rochechouart but Rödingsmarkt, and I looked up at each crossroad, wondering if I'd finally reached that Nirgend-wostrasse where Kurt, the Turk, was waiting to give me some keys, and I looked once again at my city map, so soaked now that it was splitting and falling apart . . . It was a nightmare. I was in the depths of despair . . . Except that this was no nightmare.

I'd just arrived in Hamburg, which I didn't know at all. I'd never been to Germany. Daniel had called me asking for help for the third time in a week. But this time he hadn't drawn me a bottle at sea. Instead, from the other end of the line, his almost inaudible, thin voice, so full of distress, three dots and three dashes for S.O.S. I must come, right now. I might be too late. He might die before he saw me again, that was for sure.

— Cut the crap, baby bro! You're crazy! You'll be OK!

– Please, I beg you, don't tell Ma. So she won't worry too much.

– You'll be OK. I'm on my way. You'll be fine.

But I was aware, all of a sudden, that I was saying it with no conviction. I had a hunch that fate was about to strike a second time, six months later. And I hated myself for thinking that.

It all started with feeling faint from time to time, but it hadn't worried him too much. Then he'd been found unconscious in an avenue in the Venusberg where he jogged every morning, and when he came to he saw the dazzling white ceiling of an emergency ward at the hospital.

– Damn, for a few seconds I thought I was dead! I thought that was what death is like! All white.

He'd managed to laugh it off, then he said:

– I had at least three doctors and God knows how many nurses all round me, people in green, people in red, just like on TV, you know . . .

He was still in a jokey mood when he called me two days later – to let me know things were fine, he claimed:

– I learned two words of German today: *biopsy* and *scanner*. They were talking among themselves around my bed, and I understood what they were saying: biopsy and scanner. That rang a bell.

Diagnosis two days later: rampant cirrhosis and infection of the pancreas. Then after two more days:

– Agammaglobulinemia.

– Can you spell that?

– Immuno-deficiency.

– Due to what?

No, it wasn't AIDS. But in certain types of poisoning, in certain cases when the cells are impregnated with toxic products taken in very large doses . . .

— Did you tell them you . . .?

— Yeah, yeah. Kurt's got me into a special clinic. There's a doctor who speaks good French. They know all about it. They've already dealt with athletes who . . . Well, you know the deal . . .

— Athletes who shoot themselves up with all kind of crap. Like you.

— Right.

Daniel said 'Right' with a brisk tone of defiance in his voice. He was putting on a brave front, but I felt he wouldn't hold out for long like that. And sure enough, in a fit of anxiety, he suddenly cried out:

— It's awful, Paul, it's awful! Everything's blurred, my hands are shaking, my mouth is . . . It's awful!

— We'll have to get you back home, Daniel.

— No, no, no! I'm covered here. Kurt sees to everything. But most of all, most of all, I don't want Ma to . . . I don't want Ma to . . . You understand?

— I understand. But get off the phone now.

— I don't give a fuck. It's Kurt who . . .

This Kurt who . . . This Kurt who had my brother hospital-
ized in a plush Altona clinic, this Kurt who paid for
everything. This filthy rich Kurt was Turkish, by birth,
and was actually called Adnan 'Kurt' Ventürük. But he'd
adopted as his first name his nickname 'Wolf' – *Kurt*, in
Turkish – and he'd both Germanized his surname and
given it a noble ring: von Tür. As Kurt von Tür he'd also
had his hair dyed, like my brother, and to put the finishing
touches to his whiteness he wore porcelain-blue contacts.
Daniel had cut out his photo from a brochure to show me
what he looked like: your typical good-looking Nordic
German, the thoroughbred Aryan, Hitler's fantasy. Very,
very tanned, but then . . .

The Wolf had been a champion body-builder and made
a fortune in just a few years. He owned a chain of fitness
and body-building centers, healthfood snack bars, health
stores, saunas, an FM radio station, and God knows what
else. I guessed he must also own peep shows and porn
shops and Eros centers, maybe. Once more, I preferred
not to delve any deeper. And Daniel hadn't said anything
else about him either.

Our father had been dead three months. Ma dealt with it
more bravely than we could have imagined. And Zaïa
came by the house as often as possible to take Ma's mind
off her grief. As for Daniel, oddly enough I found him
much less depressed. As if his mourning had helped him

128

to get over his usual sadness. Something had changed in him. He didn't belittle himself so much. I heard him shout out 'I'm a silly fucker! I'm a piece of shit!' less often than before. He was full of beans. Yes, full of beans.

We'd finished lunch. Ma and her sister were chatting and watching a documentary on TV about wild animals. Daniel whispered to me:

— I've got to talk to you.

We went off to his – our – bedroom. Our three-master.

— Shoot.

— I don't know where to start.

— Begin at the beginning!

He hesitated.

Me – a sudden hunch:

— You're in love?

He hesitated again, then:

— Yeah.

His breathing was loud.

Me – second hunch:

— And it's a guy . . .

My tone of voice was more accepting than questioning. A way of helping him take the leap.

He hesitated again, then with a relieved, proud smile he said:

— Yeah.

Admitting it hadn't been so hard, when it came to it. He added:

— He's German. Well, actually, he's Turkish, but he's German . . . Not a word to Ma, right? Promise!

— What do you take me for?

— It'd kill her if she knew . . .

— No, it wouldn't kill her. I don't think so. She loves

you, dammit! And as long as you're . . .

— No, but it's going to be hard enough on her when I tell her I'm . . . Because . . . well . . . I . . . I'm going to go and live in Germany. Well, I'm afraid she'll take it badly, fall apart, when I tell her.

— If you're happier there . . .

— I've got a job. A much classier thing than the Sexyshow.

— You don't say.

— Don't joke . . . Shit! There's . . . There's someone who's bought me.

— Bought you? You're not a slave, baby bro!

— No, I mean, paid for my contract. I'll be in a real show, if I want to. On a real stage . . . Not in some dive.

— Honest! You'll end up in Hollywood! Like Schwarzie . . .

I flexed my biceps and puffed up my pecs.

— Don't take the piss . . . Shit!

— Whoa, Daniel! If we can't have a laugh anymore . . . And, first off, who's this somebody?

— Well, er, the German.

— Ah, your boyfriend.

— Yeah.

— Does he have a name, your buddy?

— Kurt.

— Where does Kurt live?

— Hamburg.

— And what does Kurt do for a living?

— He's got gyms all over . . . Er . . . All sorts of stuff, you know. Healthfood bars . . . An FM radio station. He's got plenty of dough, no shit!

— So you're going to work for him . . . *For* him, or

with him – subtle difference . . .

– Well, uh . . . I don't have to work, really . . .

– Oh.

– What d'you mean, oh?

– Nothing. I just said, 'Oh.' Don't I have the right to say 'Oh' anymore? Anyway, don't mess around with me, you know damn well what I'm getting at!

– I'm not selling my ass!

– Did I say you were selling your ass? I'd just rather you didn't mess up . . . rather you didn't get burned.

– I'm old enough to . . .

– Yes. I've told you already. You're a grown-up, you can do whatever you like. But listen to me, fuck it! Listen to me! I'm asking you this because you're my brother, and Dad's gone. Go to Germany if you like, go and live there for a few days . . . check it out. Give it a try. Get it? Try it out for a week or two. And if it's all right, if you think it's the kind of life you want, then come back and tell me, and only after that go there for good. Right? If your Kurt is as flush as you say he is, he can give you a round-trip ticket, can't he? So, please, do that just for me! And if it's not OK, don't be ashamed to come back. We all make mistakes.

He accepted the deal – the first and last time that I used paternal rank, so to speak . . .

But he came back from Hamburg full of enthusiasm.

A bit ashamed, all the same, at feeling happy in the bosom of a family in mourning, and secretly sad at not being able to share his happiness with Ma. He'd opted for still hiding the real reason for his exile. Officially, for her and for Zaïa, he was going to work in a theater in

Hamburg . . . the Wollust Theater, which was owned, among others, at St Pauli on the Reeperbahn, by Kurt von Tür. But neither Ma nor Zaïa knew that St Pauli is the Pigalle of Hamburg and that *Wollust* in German means 'voluptuousness' – or 'lust'.

It was the good life in Germany! It was a great life! Real life! Kurt took him to ultra-chic clubs where, fucking hell, you left the keys of your car with the doorman, who parked it for you! Kurt had a BMW with tinted windows and a bar, and a Mercedes SLK coupé, shit, with the top that retracted automatically into the trunk! Kurt lived in a gigantic loft, almost empty, with no curtains on the huge windows, damn, with a panoramic view over the port like in movies that take place in San Francisco, and a big jacuzzi in the bathroom, which also had no curtains and was three times the size of the living room at Rue Ordener, and you wandered around butt-naked in front of infinity, the night, or in silk dressing gowns so fine that you felt almost as naked underneath as if you *were* naked . . . And when you got out of the bath, after drying off, you just threw your bath towels and bath sheets, which were changed at least three times a day, onto the floor . . . And if you felt like a fruit juice cocktail, you just had to ask the flunky, Suleyman, who was incredibly well trained, dressed all in black, and would squeeze whatever you wanted in a huge Braun juicer . . . If you wanted to listen to some music, you could choose from at least a thousand CDs; the list was on a computer, so you tapped out the title you were after and, woah, a little light flashed where the CD was on the shelf . . . And if you didn't feel like getting up from the couch, shit, man, you grabbed your mobile phone – each had his own – and you called each other at opposite ends of the loft ... It was the Thousand and One Nights!

— And what language do you speak in, from opposite ends of the loft?

— English. We get by.

— That's true. You were quite good at English at high school.

— That's what I was least bad at.

'But this isn't truth this isn't right
this isn't love this isn't life this isn't real
this is a lie'

What had most dazzled Daniel wasn't this luxury but the freedom he'd felt in Hamburg. For example: twice he'd gone for long walks at night and not a single cop had bugged him by asking for his papers. He'd taken a cab, too: well, in Germany, if you're on your own, you just sit up front, next to the driver!

'This isn't love this isn't life this isn't real
this is a lie'

He hummed these words by The Cure. He was obsessed by them. But did he know what those words meant?

No. He looked happy. And yet I was shaking for him; I was unhappy for him. He was going to go back in three or four days, and settle there. He was going back with almost no luggage. In Germany, Kurt had started to dress him. Everything was Hugo Boss! Classy, fuck it!

'This is a lie ...'

Kurt von Tür, I said to myself. The Wolf at the Gate! Master of the Theater of Lust! The Thousand and One Nights! *Alf Layla wa layla* . . . Hell, yes! Hamburg in winter, and my brother, who was about to die.

The drizzle turned to sleet, the sleet to snow. I had snow in my eyes, advancing through orange haloes, soaked to the bone, the strap of my duffel bag biting into my shoulder, my map in tatters . . . Finally I found the street, alongside the Elbe embankment, and the entrance to the building, a monumental industrial edifice, with pompous, Nazi architecture, recently converted to luxury lofts.

I rang the videophone – a camera filmed me. *Beep beep beep* . . . then the latch buzzed and the door opened.

Elevator . . . Top floor . . . Suleyman, in black silk tunic and baggy pants, made a deep bow and welcomed me inside, taking my bag.

– *Good evening, sir.*

– *Good evening, sir!*

Seeing my hair dripping, he went to fetch me a towel . . . no, a bath sheet, a huge bath sheet, thick and soft. In case I wanted to dry myself, rub myself down . . .

– Thank you.

– *Master not here*, he said in an accent that wasn't easy to decipher. *Fly to Honk Kong and Los Angeles* . . .

So saying, he handed me an envelope and a bunch of keys. The envelope contained five thousand marks in crisp new big denominations, and a letter written in a kind of pidgin English. Kurt von Tür informed me that he hadn't been able to put off a business trip. He asked me to accept his apologies, as well as the money to cover my expenses. Suleyman would fix me up in the guest room, and would be at my beck and call to help me during my stay.

No polite 'Yours most sincerely' ending, but, odder still, not a word about Daniel either!

Suleyman showed me to my room, pointing out, on the way, where the dimmer switches were. Magic: You didn't have to switch or push or even lightly touch them; you just put your hand near them . . . and halogen lights went on.

We walked across a living room that must have measured about fifty feet by forty, furnished with just three black-leather sofas. On the walls, three large pictures – black strips on a white background.

The decor in my room was every bit as sober: a bed, a low glass table, three spotlights. But the view was enchanting. The port lights were like an endless, motionless firework display. It was indeed the Thousand and One Nights!

'This isn't real . . .'

Then I remembered, because Daniel had told me as much, that on Saturdays visits to the clinic finished at six. It was five-something. If I wanted a cab, Suleyman would call one for me.

— *Ja. Danke schön.*
— *Fünf Minuten . . .*

So this was the grand life, was it? The good life? And what had the relationship between my brother and this slave-owning sultan been like? I was thinking about it in the past tense – past imperfect. I had the vague feeling that Kurt's business trip was an alibi, that this Kurt had abandoned my brother. He paid for everything because paying is the only thing that doesn't cost anything, at the end of the day. Had there been any love between them? Did they still love each other?

I remembered how my Queequeg had told me that in Germany, if you were on your own, you sat up front in a taxi, next to the driver. He saw that as the symbol of a society that was less riddled with prejudices than ours, more civilized. Slave of a sultan, but democratic!

The Mercedes joined a queue of cars crawling along the slippery Hafenstrasse, under a sign to Altona, in a whirl of snow.

The *Krankenhaus* was a cube of glass and steel.

At the reception desk, soft music wafting, and phones ringing like birdsong; and the receptionists were dressed like stewardesses.

— Er . . . Good . . . Er, *Abend* . . . Room . . . er . . . *Zimmer* . . . Panic! Couldn't remember German numbers to save my life, or the German way of making compound numbers – the opposite, it seemed to me, of Arabic. 'Eleven . . . No. *Elf* . . . Nul . . . Three . . . Name is Smaïl . . . Daniel . . .'

— Yes, Smail . . . The receptionist pointed with a pencil to our name on her screen. No dots on the i? 'Three, 0, double one, please. Third floor.'

I had permission to visit. She gave me a badge, which I had to clip to the collar of my jacket.

On the third floor, an employee gave me a package wrapped in sealed vinyl. Daniel had been put in a sterile tent and before I went into the room I had to put on rubber gloves and a white paper shirt, cover my nose and mouth with a sterilized mask, and wear a ridiculous shower cap.

— *He is very tired today*, the nurse said to me. *And, emotionally . . . So, be fast please. Ten minutes*.

She lifted the sheet of see-through plastic . . .

It was him, and yet it was no longer altogether him. It was our father. It was our grandfather. Our grandfather

137

Ahmed, who *also* died in Germany – the thought crossed my mind. And the horror, the shame, the sickness of having had such a thought. *Heichma*!

A Koran in French lay on the bedside table, next to a CD Walkman and a pile of raï CDs . . .

– Paul.

– Daniel.

– So, here we are.

– So, here we are. My poor Queequeg!

The paper mask muffled my words, dulling and stifling them.

Daniel smiled at me. I said to myself, inside, that I mustn't cry in front of him, and again: I mustn't cry in front of him, I mustn't cry in front of him.

– Does it hurt?

– Not any more.

(Not any more.)

– Then you're getting better!

– Or worse.

(Or worse.)

– Kurt's gone off to . . .

– Kurt hasn't been to see me since they put me in this tent.

– Oh.

(Oh.)

I quickly had to find something lighthearted to say, a joke . . . Or else the tears would flow.

– 'The Arabs will live in tents, the heirs of Ismaël . . .' Abraham wished it so: the people of Ismaël will be a nomadic people . . . The Smaïls! D'you remember what Mr Hamel explained to me, and then I told you? By his handmaiden Agar, Abraham had a natural son out of wedlock: Ismaël. Then, by Sara, he had a legitimate son: Israël. Ismaël and Israël played together. But Sara was jealous, and didn't want her son to play with the son of a handmaiden. So she asked Abraham to send Agar and Ismaël into the desert . . . Where we had . . . I mean, where they nearly died of thirst.

His eyes lit up. It was like the old days when I would read him stories before the light went out – before getting the ship ready for the night, before hoisting the sails for the great voyage of sleep.

He said to me:

– You promised, when we got back from the cemetery, remember? You promised you'd start writing a book.

– Yes, I promised.

– You'd better get down to it.

– Yes. And you, you'd better get better.

He died a week later. At about eleven in the morning. I was there. Or rather . . . I was in the corridor. When they asked me, at about 10.30, to leave the room, I'd already understood.

– *Er hat nicht geleiden.*

How could she be sure he hadn't suffered? Had she *put him to sleep?*

The burial – I'm talking about our father's burial. I've gone back a few pages in my notebook, and Daniel was cremated without ceremony, without witnesses, with just his brother there. Even though Kurt had got back from his business trip the day before, he didn't want to be there – the funeral at the Thiais cemetery was what you'd call a nice funeral. A chance for people to get together, a reunion for family and friends . . . Emotion and dignity.

There was – yes – a feeling of peace, almost. I didn't feel any more rebellion inside me. The sky was very blue, and birds sang in the foliage ('Wow, mofo, foliage, conceited prick! Asshole!').

When we reached the Muslim neighborhood, Ma, Zaïa, Daniel and I got out of the funeral car and went on on foot. Between her two grown sons holding her by the elbows, Ma stood very straight and didn't stumble on the gravel on the path.

We walked alongside the spot reserved for Muslim soldiers from North Africa, the rows of simple slabs, all the same, in a half-circle, engraved with the first names of all those young men who'd died for France, our brothers: Saïd, Mohamed, Rabah, Abdelkader, Rachid, Djeloul, Tahar, and so on. Farther on, in a communal grave, victims of the bloody night of October 17, 1961, were buried.

It was a big procession. Behind us came cousins, cousins of cousins, cousins of cousins of cousins – I hadn't known we were such a big tribe. Then our friends,

Daniel's and mine. Diop, old Mr Hamel . . . Lastly, my
father's colleagues, who had offered a large wreath
dedicated very simply *To Yacine*.

When it was all over, everybody offered to take us
back to Rue Ordener. A distant cousin, whose first name I
hadn't known until then, offered to take us in his car, a
Renault Espace. He had arranged the seats facing each
other in the back, and he said, with a smug little smile:

— It's just like a small living room. You'll be better off
with me. Get in!

So there we were, facing each other, Ma, Zaïa, Daniel,
and me.

Our teeth stayed clenched. Even Zaïa was unable to say
the slightest word. We had to drive right across Paris, and
the streets were very busy. The road home seemed to
take forever. Huge traffic jam on Boulevard de Magenta,
deafening concert of horns . . .

As had happened often of late, there'd been trouble at
the Barbès-Rochechouart intersection. Identity checks?
Demo for illegals? Spontaneous defense of some thieves
who'd just been arrested? Rival gangs of dealers settling
scores? Fighting between rival groups of fundamentalists?
A roundup of ethnic types? We didn't know what it was:
the Espace was at a standstill by the Luxor, and we looked
on without understanding. People were running in all
directions, shouting . . . Police sirens drowned out wailing
women. A line of police buses appeared. Riot police
jumped out before they'd stopped, to get to the scene
that much faster.

In front of Tati,* clutching their truncheons, they

* A down-market department store

started to charge the crowd indiscriminately.

For a split second, for my brother and for me, our hatred prevailed over our despair. From the depths of his sadness, Daniel uttered a vague:

— Cocksuckers!

And me:

— The bastards! The bastards!

Every day, for several weeks, they'd been finding bodies of Arabs drowned in the Seine and St Martin's Canal. Others were found in woods around Paris, at Chaville and Meudon. Men who had been killed with a bullet in the belly, or strangled with their own ties or a length of wire. They had neither ID papers nor money on them. Several hundred had disappeared like this in the autumn of 1961: FMA, French Muslims from Algeria, or simply NA, North Africans. Like my uncle Mehdi.

In full daylight, an unmarked Peugeot 403 would pull up level with a poor guy who had 'the features'. Plain-clothes inspectors would make him get in, and would then tear away at top speed . . . He would never be seen again alive.

Massive swoops and raids took place every night. Armed with long truncheons and submachine guns, police officers went Arab-bashing in subways, Arab-bashing at Maison-Blanche, Arab-bashing at the Goutte d'Or. On the Asnières and Gennevilliers bridges, they stopped buses and sorted through the passengers. On one side, people of 'European type', on the other the 'Fellouzes',* whom they shipped straight off. Or ten or twelve of them would burst into a café used by 'Nor'Afs' and break the place up. People were tortured in police

* A term describing Algerian soldiers during the Algerian War of Independence (1954–62)

143

stations and detention centers.

On October 5, the French government introduced a curfew for all French Muslims from Algeria. Arabs, whether Algerian or not, lived in a state of fear. Italians and Portuguese guys were murdered simply because they looked 'the type' . . . But on the seventeenth the National Liberation Front – the FLN – put out the word for everyone to demonstrate peacefully and to demand that the curfew be lifted. The demonstrators were unarmed, and most of them were dressed to the nines, as if at a party. Then the terrible slaughter started.

At home, I only heard people talking about it on three or four occasions, and then only in veiled terms. As if my parents were ashamed of what went down, as if it was up to *them* to feel ashamed. Zaïa spoke more openly about it, but in hushed tones, too. I got to know a bit more about it from Mr Hamel, who finally admitted to me that, at that time, he was part of a support network for the FLN. And four or five years ago, a book titled *The Battle of Paris* came out detailing the full horror of that *Kristallnacht*.

At the Ile de la Cité, fifty men were massacred in a yard at the police headquarters. In the Sports Arena, at the Porte de Versailles, of the six thousand rounded up, many were seriously injured, left unattended, with nothing to drink, stripped of what paltry possessions they had – their watches, their wallets – by the cops, who shared out the loot . . . And they were finished off with rifle butts when they still had enough courage left to raise their voices and chant: 'Freedom! Freedom!'

As I said, my uncle was off to work back stage at the Olympia. (Jacques Brel was on the program that night.

Zaïa has kept a photo of the singer dedicated *To my friend Mehdi*.) His corpse was fished out at the main sewer at Conflans Ste-Honorine on October 21 . . . or October 22.

Across the file at the forensic science laboratory, somebody had scrawled, in big red letters, SUICIDE – apparently.

Today, as I write these lines, I realize that when he died he was the age I am today: twenty-seven. Zaïa was twenty-three. Leïla – Ma – fourteen.

The chief of police at the time was Maurice Papon, who's since been found guilty of crimes against humanity – but not for those goings-on.

On the TV news one night, when they were debating whether to charge him, his face appeared, and I saw my father, usually so reserved, so measured in his feelings, grimacing with hatred, get up from the table, stick two fingers at the screen simulating a pistol, aim, get even closer until he was actually touching the screen, and fire at point-blank range.

– *Halouf*!

The apartment is empty, and it echoes. On the floor and the walls, the signs of furniture removed. In the children's bedroom, the ghostlike presence of our bunk beds conjures up more than ever our ship becalmed in the mist, Daniel and me – 'We're not leaving!'

Among odd papers that tumbled from a drawer during the move, a notebook, an advertisement for a failsafe method of intensive body-building – *before and after* – pages ripped from a schoolbook scattered on the floor. I come on this, in my handwriting, which I guess I wrote coming back from a visit to Mr Hamel – though I don't remember it:

> *I'm an Arab. Doesn't an Arab have two eyes? Doesn't an Arab have hands, organs, proportions, senses, feelings, and passions? Doesn't he eat the same food, isn't he wounded by the same weapons, liable to have the same illnesses, cured by the same remedies, made hot or cold by the same summer and winter as a born and bred Frenchman?*

Shakespeare revised and corrected by me *myself*! I wasn't afraid of anything. If someone asked me if I knew what I was going to be when I grew up, I would say: 'A writer.'

I stoop to pick up a little Playmobil figure that's been overlooked: the Red Cross ambulance driver with his first-aid kit.

Diop and Pinocchio call me from the landing:

— What the fuck are you up to, Paulou?

— Paulou! Damn, man! What are you doing?

No, no sentimentality! The three of us still have to take the furniture Ma wanted to keep – her bed, an armchair, a wardrobe with a full-length mirror, and a Moroccan chest – upstairs to my aunt Zaïa, who lives on the fifth floor, no elevator. The rest, the dining-room suite, the household gadgets, the bunk beds, and the little boat desks have all been sold off. Zaïa has persuaded her sister to come and live with her. Ma would die of sadness if she stayed on her own any longer at Rue Ordener, and since she was having more and more trouble paying the rent and since her surviving son had decided to go and live in Morocco . . . Where they would join him, maybe, the two of them, once he'd settled in.

— Paulououou!

— Coming! *Leave taking with affection and new noises*!

— What?

— Rimbaud.

Diop, Pinocchio and I all collapse onto the sofa, dripping, and pass the jug of iced water and the barley water from one to the other – real barley water made by Zaïa. The move is over. On the sideboard, Ma has already arranged some of her things among my aunt's souvenirs: a portrait of my father, his work medal, one of their wedding photos, Daniel in class one, just learning how to read, and me in the top class at primary school, Daniel and me on the beach, Daniel aged fourteen or fifteen, still very puny but posing for the camera like Mr Muscle.

Through the kitchen door, ajar, I can see the two sisters busying themselves. They're cooking up a storm for us three volunteer furniture-movers, and it'll double as a farewell supper for me. While they fold sheets of filo pastry, gently stirring the tajine with a wooden spoon, rolling the couscous between their fingers, they chatter merrily in Arabic . . . Better still, they're laughing! I suddenly hear them burst into peals of laughter.

After supper, I'll go home and finish packing my bags, turn off the taps and the meter. I'll give the keys back to Mr Zeboudji. It'll be a long time before I see *You'll always find bargains at Berber*! again. I'll spend my last night in France here on this sofa, under the portrait of my uncle Mehdi. My flight's tomorrow.

Next day, I'd been cunning enough to cut my goodbyes short. I pretended I hadn't read my ticket properly. The flight leaves at 1.30 p.m., instead of 3.30, as I'd originally thought. I didn't want to watch Ma sobbing too long.

Diop came with me to Orly. There was a knot in my throat, but he seemed even more upset than me.

— Get going! I said to him. I hate kissing and hugging in public.

I just laid a hand on his shoulder.

Once through passport control, I turned round and saw him brandishing the James Baldwin book he'd forgotten to give back to me: *The Fire Next Time*.

I motioned to him to keep it: a present.

In my take-on bag I had the urn containing Daniel's ashes. I'd put it on the conveyor belt through the metal detector. The customs policewoman called me over and got me to open the bag:

— What's this?

I'd anticipated the question. I answered by brandishing the papers I'd needed to bring the ashes into France:

— A funeral urn. Here are all the *relevant* documents.

(*Relevant* was the word I used! An A-rab, but an educated A-rab.)

This didn't stop her asking me to open it, though. I protested, and my tone of voice grew louder: No, I'm not going to open it. She said I must. I said it was an infringement of my human rights and my dignity, and showed a lack of respect for the rights of the deceased. I also pointed out to her that it was rare for anyone to try and smuggle drugs or explosives through in this direction. Her colleague, looking embarrassed, called their superior on his walkie-talkie. I could see the moment coming when I would no longer be able to board my flight. Curious passengers gave me dirty looks. (The fire, next time!)

I had to wait. They were trying to contact the captain.

If you're continually suspicious of us, aren't we going to take offence? If you talk down to us, isn't that going to annoy us? If you ask us for our papers for the slightest thing, aren't we going to become exasperated? If you treat us like wogs, ragheads and A-rabs, isn't that humiliating for us? If you beat the shit out of us in police stations, doesn't this hurt us? If you kick us and break our fingers when you take us into custody, if you spit – quite literally – in our faces, if you piss on us – quite literally . . . And if you refuse to give us jobs that you'll give to others who are less qualified but less swarthy, too, won't we finally rise up in revolt? Doesn't an Arab have feelings, emotions, and passions? If we're like you in every other way, we'll be like you in this, too: We'll get our revenge.

The captain of Royal Air Maroc flight AT761 was called Idir Ben Achab – cross my heart, I'm not making it up. He gave me permission to board without opening the urn.

I suddenly thought back to a comedy routine that always made my father laugh until he cried when he heard it on the radio. It had to do with a lower-middle-class French couple going on vacation to Morocco and seeing – horror of horrors! – that even the steward was

150

an Arab! And even the captain was an Arab! And even the king there was an Arab!

I can hear him laughing now.

I don't know if I'm right or wrong. I haven't got a clue what's in store for me over there. Whether I'll have a new, more beautiful life, or whether I'll quickly get the feeling I've made a big mistake. But it'll be my fuck-up, my choice. And I'll go along with the consequences, and I think I'll even be proud of what I've done. I may go back to France in a few weeks, or months, with no illusions left . . . But what illusions? I haven't got any. I know it'll be just as difficult in Morocco, but in a different way. I'm setting off on an adventure, that's all. So be it.

Weigh anchor! Cast off! Furl the foresails! Lower the spanker! Hoist the jib and the flying jib! Hug the wind! Hug the wind! Ready about! Heave-ho! Haul in the sails! Furl! Luff! Headwind . . . 'We remind you there is no smoking on board. We ask that you fasten your seat belt, and make sure that your seat and the tray in front of you have been returned to the upright position . . .' *Irbitou ah zimato-koum* . . . Takeoff in two minutes . . . *Inch' Allah*!